DARWIN SPEAKS!

DARWIN SPEAKS!

GARY CLEMENTS

GAC

To my children, Melanie, Nicola, and Cameron,
with gratitude for their love and support.

And, of course, to Darwin,
for his inspiration and companionship.

Chapter 1

Darwin on Life
Episode 1: Darwin's First Words

[Opening theme music]

VO: *Darwin on Life*: Man and dog at the dawn of a new age.

Walker Grant: Hello, and welcome to my podcast, *Darwin on Life*. I am your host, Walker Grant. Listeners, today is a historic day.

But before I tell you why, I need to give you a little background. For the past year, I have been loading thousands of hours of recordings of canine communication into a specially adapted artificial intelligence or AI program. These recordings consist of vocalizations made by dogs as they interact with other dogs and with humans. The AI program analyzed this material and converted these sounds into human speech. The program is also able to translate human speech into sounds that dogs can understand.

This promises to be an incredible breakthrough in interspecies communication, and I want the world, or at least the listeners of this podcast, to be able to hear for themselves the first intelligible conversation between man and dog. I have invited Darwin, my pet beagle, to join me in this experiment. Darwin and I are both wearing headphones, so you will not be able to hear the canine vocalizations, just the "human"—I am making little air quotes here around "human"—speech.

OK, here we go. This is so exciting! Darwin, can you hear me?

Hmm, let me make sure the app is running. Seems to be working. I'll try again.

Darwin, can you—

Darwin: Pathetic.

WG: Oh my God. He spoke! Wait a minute. Darwin, did you say—

Darwin: Of course I can hear you. We are sitting only three feet apart. I may be red–green color blind, but I'm not deaf.

WG: Oh, right. But did I hear you correctly? Was the first thing you said "pathetic"?

Darwin: No, the first thing I said was "Mama," but that was a couple of years ago when I was a young pup. The first thing I said to you that you understood was "pathetic." I am making little air quotes here.

WG: I see. But why did you say "pathetic"?

Darwin: Because that's what you are. You said yourself that this was a historic occasion. But the most profound thing you could think of to say as the first words understood between man and dog was "Darwin, can you hear me?" I mean, you might as well have said, "Hey, Darwin, looks like rain, eh?" or "Darwin, how about kibble for lunch?"

WG: Uh, I guess you're right. I should have given it more thought.

Darwin: That's for sure. But look, don't be too hard on yourself. All of you so-called geniuses are the same. Do you know what Alexander Graham Bell said the first time he spoke into the telephone?

WG: No, I don't think so.

Darwin: He said, "Mr. Watson, come here. I want to see you." Can you imagine anything more banal?

WG: That is pretty vanilla.

Darwin: Edison was just as bad. Do you think the first thing he recorded on his new phonograph was something classy like Hamlet's soliloquy or Lincoln's Gettysburg Address? No. He just started reciting "Mary Had a Little Lamb." That hardly counts as a light bulb moment.

WG: Hmm. I guess it was the first thing that popped into his head.

Darwin: Business tycoons can be just as bad. One night, hotel mogul Conrad Hilton...you do know who Conrad Hilton was, don't you?

WG: Not really.

Darwin: Paris Hilton's great-grandfather. Does that help?

WG: Ah, sure.

Darwin: Anyway, Conrad Hilton was on *The Tonight Show* one night, and the host, Johnny Carson, asked him if he had a message for the American people. Here was a chance to say something truly meaningful to the millions of Johnny's loyal viewers. Hilton looked serious for a moment, then turned to the camera and said, "Please put the shower curtain inside the tub!" Can you believe it?

WG: Wow, what a lost opportunity!

Darwin: I'll say. About the only person who got the famous-first-words thing right was Neil Armstrong when he stepped on the moon: "That's one small step for a man, one giant leap for mankind." Now that was something worth saying!

WG: Look, Darwin, I'm sorry I messed up our first conversation.

Darwin: That's OK. As we dogs say, "To err is human; to forgive, canine."

WG: That's a dog quote? It sounds a little derivative to me.

Darwin: It's not derivative; it's an improvement over the original.

WG: If you say so. But, hey, this is exciting, isn't it? I've always wondered what was going on inside your head. Now everything is clear.

Darwin: I'm not sure why it wasn't clear before. After all, I only ever try to communicate three things to you. If I'm hungry, I bark. If I want to cuddle, I cry. If I want a chew toy, I howl. What's so hard about that?

WG: I guess I did have that figured out. Hey, what do you say when you want to go outside to do your business?

Darwin: I don't say anything. Why would I ask for that? You're the only one who gets upset when I pee in the house. It's no fur off my butt; I can go anywhere.

WG: So I've noticed. Is "no fur off my butt" another one of your improvements on common sayings?

Darwin: Precisely. You're starting to catch on.

WG: Darwin, I must say I am pleasantly surprised at what a large vocabulary you have. And you seem to know a lot of interesting stuff. How did you learn so many words? And where did you get all this information?

Darwin: I suppose I have you to thank for that. You leave the TV on all day, even when you are not watching it. It took me only a few months to learn to speak English.

WG: You mean you were able to understand what the people on TV were saying? That's incredible!

Darwin: Well, you don't exactly watch a lot of highbrow entertainment. I mean, how hard is it to understand, "I hope Calvin gives me the rose," or "Pat, I'd like to buy a vowel." Thank God for *Jeopardy!* That's where I pick up most of my general knowledge.

WG: I guess I should up my TV game. From now on, I'll try to mix in a little more History Channel and Discovery. Would you like that?

Darwin: Yes, I would. And some Animal Planet would be nice, too, please.

WG: In case they have a show about dogs?

Darwin: I know about dogs. What I could use would be information that helps me stay one step ahead of predators.

WG: Predators? What predators?

Darwin: You know, jackals, alligators, sharks—they all have a strong hankering for fresh dog meat.

WG: Uh, OK. But seriously, Darwin, I don't think you have anything to fear from predators around here. This is a nice, safe residential neighborhood. I can assure you there are no jackals, alligators, or sharks roaming the streets.

Darwin: That's what you think. But as we dogs say, "Forewarned is foreclawed."

WG: "Forewarned is fore—" Oh, I get it. Well, Darwin, this has been a remarkable beginning to our little experiment, but I think we should save something for future podcasts. Before we sign off, is there anything you would like to say? Something a little more profound than "Darwin, can you hear me?"

Darwin: Ditch the leash!

WG: Ditch the leash? What do you mean?

Darwin: Ditch the leash! Dogs were meant to run free. Down with human tyranny! Down with the oppression of canines! *Vive les chiens! ¡Viva los perros!*

WG: Wait a minute. You speak French and Spanish, too?

Darwin: *Bien sûr. Por supuesto.* We dogs are sophisticated polyglots.

WG: Polliwogs?

Darwin: Polyglots! We dogs speak several languages, human and animal. It is a travesty that we have to be chained to our human so-called masters. If anyone should be the masters, it should be us.

WG: Well, Darwin, it looks like we have a lot to discuss. But for now, let's just say goodbye to our podcast listeners and ask them to tune in to the next episode of *Darwin on Life.* Goodbye!

Darwin: [Singing] So long, farewell, *auf Wiedersehen, adieu. Adieu, Adieu,* to you and you and you...

[Outro music; credits]

Chapter 2

October 12, 2023

OH MY GOD! This has been the best day of my life! All my hard work has paid off beyond my wildest expectations. All my craziest dreams of scientific achievement have come true. I have been pinching myself all day just to be sure I'm not dreaming. I knew in my heart that humans and animals could communicate on a much deeper level, but I never expected to have such an intelligent conversation with my own dog.

This must be how Einstein felt when he put the theory of relativity down on paper for the first time. This must be how Neil Armstrong felt when he first stepped foot on the moon. Darwin was right, though—I should have thought of something more momentous to say during our first exchange of words. Still, this is a breakthrough of enormous proportions.

My goodness, I might even get a Nobel Prize! But which category? I guess physiology would be the best match, but that prize usually goes to someone who has cured a disease. I'll have to see if there is an award for achievement in interspecies communication. I'll do a Google search first thing tomorrow. At the very least, I should be able to convince the knuckle-draggers in the university's human resources department to give me a full-time position. In fact, they should grant me full tenure immediately. Who else on the faculty has done anything like what I have done? No one, that's who!

But I'm getting ahead of myself. I still have a lot of work to do. Although, I am amazed at how quickly Darwin and I were able to have a fluid conversation. I thought it would take months for him to adapt to the setup. And I never imagined he would demonstrate so much intelligence and subtlety in his conversation at this early stage. I have to rethink my work plan and speed things up considerably.

I also need to rethink my relationship with Darwin. I had no idea he was able to understand what I have been saying to him all these months. I hope I haven't said anything hurtful or insulting. Now that I think of it, I was probably a little hard on him during his early house training. He was still pretty young then, so I hope he has forgotten all of that. He did take a somewhat snarky tone with me during our conversation. Maybe he has been harboring a lot of built-up resentment and just let it all out when he had the chance.

Shoot, he must think I'm an idiot for lavishing praise on him every time he pees and poops or eats his dog food. I mean, that's how you encourage a young child to do the right thing. So I'm told, anyway; I don't have any experience with young children. But Darwin clearly operates at a very high intellectual level, so he might find it demeaning to be rewarded for such elementary behavior.

Damn, it just occurred to me that Darwin knows everything there is to know about me, and that he now has the power to tell the world what he knows. Not that I have anything to be ashamed of, but nobody wants every detail of their persomal life exposed to the public. I will have a talk with him to make sure we agree on maintaining our privacy. I really don't want to have to give up the podcast. It seems like the best way to bring my research to a wider public. They say that a man's best friend is his dog, and that dogs are loyal to a fault. Of course, it's just people who say that. I wonder what Darwin thinks.

I have started this journal mostly to have a record of my experiments. I will, however, include some personal reflections to show how my own thinking advances during the course of this research. Perhaps, someday, a science historian will find it useful to trace the development of what I hope will be a greater understanding of animal cognition. At the very least, it should help me remember what topics I want to address with Darwin during our conversations.

October 13, 2023

I didn't have much luck finding an appropriate reward for my research, but I did make an appointment to speak with the head of personnel at the university. I realize I'm rather far along in my career to be seeking a tenured position, but I hope the administration will recognize that my work is of unusual value and not take my age too much into consideration.

I also spoke to Darwin. As I feared, he had a long laundry list of complaints. It was things that all pet owners do and say, but it was enlightening—and more than a little humbling—to hear about it from a dog's perspective. He was more bemused than insulted by my compliments on his eating and eliminating. But he takes great exception to being treated like, well, like a dog. Nevertheless, he seemed to be willing to carry on with the podcast. He didn't outright promise not to say anything embarrassing about me, but I think it's worth the risk to keep working together.

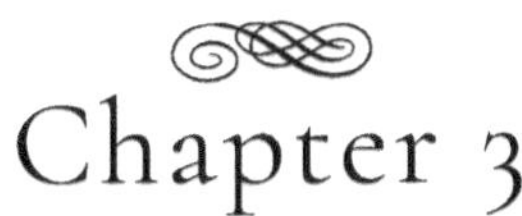

Chapter 3

Darwin on Life
Episode 2: How Darwin Got His Name

[Opening theme music]

VO: *Darwin on Life*: Man and dog at the dawn of a new age.

Walker Grant: Hello, again. This is your host, Walker Grant. As I explained in episode one, I have invented an app that uses artificial intelligence to translate the sounds that dogs make into human speech. It also translates human speech into sounds that dogs can understand. As we discovered in the first episode, however, this is unnecessary with Darwin, my pet beagle, as he learned to understand English by watching a lot of TV.

So, Darwin, good day. What do you say we pick up our conversation again? There is so much I want to know about how dogs think. Would you like that?

Darwin: I guess so. I hope it won't take too long, though. I really need a nap.

WG: A nap? Seems to me you spend about twenty hours a day sleeping. In fact, that's something I wanted to ask you about. Why do dogs spend so much time snoozing?

Darwin: First of all, let's get one thing straight. I am a dog, but I don't claim to represent all dogs. Each dog is an individual with his own needs, tastes, and viewpoints. It's like if I were to ask you, "Why do humans spend so much time picking their noses?"

WG: Humans don't spend a lot of time picking their noses.

Darwin: Well, excuse me. The only human I have been able to observe at close range is you. And you certainly spend a lot of time picking your nose. So, I just assumed—

WG: I do not spend a lot of time picking my nose! Can we please get back to the topic of sleep?

Darwin: Fine. But that brings me to my second point. What you call "sleeping" is what we dogs call "strategic energy conservation sessions" or SECS. When we dogs have SECS, we are just preparing ourselves for possible encounters with predators.

WG: I don't understand. Why would you have sex to prepare for an encounter with a predator?

Darwin: Not sex, you pervert! SECS. S, E, C, S; strategic energy conservation sessions. Have you even heard a word I have been saying?

WG: Oh, sorry. But you must admit that is a confusing acronym.

Darwin: Not to us dogs.

WG: And I still don't understand your preoccupation with predators. Why do you feel so threatened?

Darwin: If you actually watched the news, instead of using it as just background noise, you would understand the perils we dogs face. Did you not see the story about the black bear that broke through a backyard fence to try to steal some food? If it wasn't for the courageous cocker spaniel who raised the alarm, who knows what tragedy would have transpired?

WG: I guess I must have missed that one.

Darwin: Or how about the bald eagle who swooped down to try to carry off a poor little chihuahua? Fortunately, the chihuahua ducked under the porch at the last moment. We dogs have to be on our paws every second in order to stay safe. That's why we nap so often—to make sure we have the energy we need in times of crisis.

WG: OK, you may have a point.

Darwin: I suppose you never noticed that I usually have one eye open when I am resting.

WG: Actually, I have noticed that, and I find it a bit creepy. I guess I assumed that you were constantly on the lookout for food falling on the floor.

Darwin: From your snippy tone, it seems you think I am some kind of a glutton.

WG: Well, you do seem to be very food-focused. When you're in the kitchen, you lick up the tiniest of crumbs off the floor. And when we go for our walks, you seem to be always sniffing around for something to eat—usually something disgusting like deer poop.

Darwin: Are you sure you want to go down this road? I have seen some of the stuff you eat, and the word disgusting barely begins to describe it. Fatty, salty snacks with no nutritional value. Sports drinks in colors not found in nature. How you manage to stay alive is a mystery to me.

WG: OK, I admit my diet is not always the best. But don't I give you enough good food to eat? I mean, you get three meals a day, and when I go out, I always leave you a chew toy filled with peanut butter and kibble.

Darwin: You must understand that we dogs are natural scavengers. It is in our DNA to be constantly on the prowl for food. Don't forget, we have been domesticated for only a few thousand years. We still have the instincts of our wolf ancestors.

WG: Hmm. I would have thought that instinct would have died out by now.

Darwin: You humans have had handkerchiefs for hundreds of years, yet you still pick your noses.

WG: OK, OK, can we declare a truce? I won't complain about your scavenging if you stop commenting on nose picking. Deal?

Darwin: Deal.

WG: Thank you. Oh, there's something else I wanted to ask you. Do you know why I called you Darwin?

Darwin: Let me guess. Charles Darwin, the guy who came up with the theory of evolution, explored the Galapagos Islands on a ship called HMS *Beagle*. So, you thought it would be cute to call your beagle Darwin.

WG: Wow, that's right! You really are remarkably well-informed. Even some of my cleverest friends don't make the connection until I point it out to them.

Darwin: So, what you're saying is that you gave your highly intelligent and well-informed canine companion a joke name. Nice.

WG: Gosh, when you put it that way, it does seem that I was a bit insensitive. Would you like me to change your name?

Darwin: Don't bother. All the names you humans come up with sound stupid to us dogs.

WG: Do dogs have names for each other? Like, when we run into Rex and Daisy on our morning walk, do you greet them with a dog name?

Darwin: As I'm sure you have noticed, when we dogs greet each other, it is less about talking and more about smelling. Because of our poor eyesight, we don't necessarily recognize each other until we have a chance to give each other a good sniff. Our sense of smell is so refined that we can identify thousands of other dogs just by their individual odor.

So, we don't give each other names in the same sense that you humans do. Besides, human names are based largely on family connections. Since you humans separate us from our families at a young age, a naming system based on family ties wouldn't make sense for us dogs. Therefore, we have developed a system based on our unique fragrances.

WG: I see. But how exactly does that work?

Darwin: There is no way to explain it in a way that you would understand. The best I can do is by analogy. Take the dog you call Rex. The two principal strains in his unique fragrance are sandalwood and decayed pumpkin. So, in human language, you would call him Sandalwood Decayed Pumpkin.

WG: That is fascinating! So, should I call Rex by his dog name, Sandalwood Decayed Pumpkin, the next time I see him?

Darwin: If you do, I will bite you very hard in a very sensitive place.

WG: Why? That's his name, isn't it?

Darwin: I said that was an analogy to a human name that captures his essence. It would be very offensive to him to actually call him by those human words.

WG: OK. I will stick with Rex. But if you don't mind me asking, what would be the analogous name that you go by?

Darwin: I do mind you asking. I don't trust you not to use it.

WG: Hmm. Must be something embarrassing. Since you dogs greet each other by sniffing your private parts, I am guessing that most of the names involve unpleasant body odors. Am I right?

Darwin: I am really starting to regret agreeing to talk about this. For your information, dogs' odors are not the least bit unpleasant to us. The wide range of scents available to our sense of smell is a source of endless delight. It's like the way you listen to classical music to enjoy the wide range of notes and the multiple instruments in a symphony orchestra. The same way that hearing a familiar voice is pleasing to you humans, we dogs get a warm feeling when we smell an old friend.

WG: You know, I really am learning a lot from you, Darwin. I can't wait to dig into some other topics in future episodes. Before you head off for your nap, I'd like to ask you a couple more questions. Do you dogs have names for us humans based on the same system of individual odors?

Darwin: Of course. Why else would we sniff humans when we greet them?

WG: Good point. Just out of curiosity, then, what would be the analogous human name for how you refer to me?

Darwin: Are you sure you want to know? Do you promise not to be offended?

WG: Sure. What is it?

Darwin: Boogers Junk Food. I call you Booger for short.

WG: Fair enough. Enjoy your nap, or your SECS as you call it, and we will talk again soon.

Darwin: [Sound of snoring].

[Outro music; credits]

Chapter 4

October 21, 2023

My meeting with the head of the personnel committee, Dr. Gabor from the physics department, did not go as well as I had hoped. I brought recordings of the two episodes of the *Darwin on Life* podcast so that she could hear for herself what a startling breakthrough I had made. She listened to the first episode with a bemused expression on her face, but when I started to play the second episode, she told me she had heard enough. Naturally, I thought she was about to offer me a tenured position right there on the spot. Instead, she reminded me that applications would not be accepted for another few months and directed me to the university's job list webpage for further information.

I asked her what she thought of the podcast, and, with a slight smirk, she said she found it rather amusing. She then ushered me out of her office.

I stood for several minutes in the hallway pondering what had just happened. "Amusing?" I asked myself. Sure, some of Darwin's comments were made in the kind of world-weary, cynical tone that a lot of faculty members equate with humor. But how could she not see the bigger picture? How was it that she was not blown away by the fact that, for the first time in human history, a man was able to have an intelligent, comprehensible conversation with a representative of another species?

She must have thought the recording was a put-on. She probably thinks I faked Darwin's dialogue and was just playing some kind of practical joke on her. I am going to have to do a better job of documenting my work so I will be ready when hiring season comes around.

I have to say, the second podcast episode was in some ways more remarkable than the first. I'll admit I was a bit annoyed by Darwin's focus on nose picking. But it was fascinating to see how aware he is of the differences between human and canine approaches to issues, and how these can be traced to the different biological and cultural factors that influence the two species. This is exactly the kind of information I was hoping to glean from my experiments with interspecies communication. In the coming episodes, I will try to draw Darwin out on these divergent perspectives.

Now that I think of it, perhaps all Dr. Gabor was trying to tell me was that I need to flesh out these research findings before I can make a strong case for myself as tenure-worthy. Sure, a few canine insights are interesting, but a full-blown analysis of the dichotomy between dog-think and human-think would be a major contribution to our understanding of the differences between the two species.

Or maybe she was just jealous that she had never come up with a discovery quite so thrilling as mine. Universities are rife with this kind of petty competitiveness, especially between the so-called hard sciences like physics and chemistry and the soft sciences like psychology and communications studies. In any case, I will be better prepared next time.

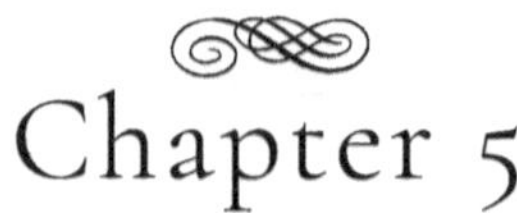# Chapter 5

Darwin on Life
Episode 3: Darwin for President!

[Opening theme music]

VO: *Darwin on Life*: Man and dog at the dawn of a new age.

Walker Grant: Hey, everyone! Welcome back to *Darwin on Life*, the podcast where my beagle, Darwin, and I talk to each other through the magic of artificial intelligence. I am your host, Walker Grant, and today I thought Darwin and I could chat about his daily routine—when he gets up, what he eats, when he goes out—

Darwin: B-o-o-o-ring.

WG: Hey, Darwin, I was just about to introduce you. How are you today?

Darwin: Bored.

WG: Bored? I'm sorry to hear that. Maybe once we get into the conversation, you will find it more interesting.

Darwin: I doubt it. You said you wanted to talk about my routine. Routine is synonymous with boring. Why would anyone be interested in hearing about that?

WG: Hmm. Maybe you're right. Is there something you would rather talk about?

Darwin: Politics.

WG: Politics? What do you know about politics?

Darwin: What does anyone know about politics? It all seems like smoke and mirrors most of the time. But I am a bit of a newshound, so I am quite up-to-date on the issues.

WG: Oh, right. I forgot how much television you watch.

Darwin: And I listen to the radio. Thank goodness you keep it tuned to NPR. If I had to listen to talk radio all day, I think I would go mad.

WG: Yeah, it can get kind of wacky. So, since you are so *au courant* with the political news, who are you favoring in the presidential race?

Darwin: I haven't made up my mind yet.

WG: Well, what do you think of Joe Biden?

Darwin: On the plus side, Biden has dogs, so he must be a generally good and wise man. On the other hand, he has banned the dogs from the White House just because they got a little too playful.

WG: Playful? They bit members of his Secret Service detail several times. You call that playful?

Darwin: I'm sure it was all a misunderstanding. The agents probably did something stupid, like picking up their chew toys or getting between the dogs and their food bowls. Dogs rarely bite unless provoked.

WG: Maybe. How about Donald Trump? Does he appeal to you?

Darwin: Trump doesn't seem to be a dog lover. He was the first president in decades not to have a dog in the White House. And he doesn't seem to have a very high opinion of dogs. When he talks about his political enemies, he uses a lot of expressions like "choked like a dog," "barked like a dog," "sweated like a dog," and "lied like a dog." I think he likes dogs about as much as he likes immigrants. So, I would be reluctant to vote for him.

WG: You do know that dogs do not have the right to vote, don't you?

Darwin: Don't remind me. It's just another example of human oppression of canines. I'm sure if dogs had the vote, we would have much better leaders in office.

WG: We couldn't have much worse. So then, what are the issues that are most important to you in the upcoming election: the economy, the wars in Ukraine and Gaza, women's reproductive rights?

Darwin: Leash laws.

WG: Leash laws?

Darwin: That's right, leash laws. They should all be repealed. What right do you humans have to control our liberty? It's a violation of the constitutional ban on cruel and unusual punishment. None of us dogs has even been convicted of a crime, so there is no justification for restricting our freedom. It's time to ditch the leash!

WG: Darwin, I understand that this is an important issue for you. But you have to look at it from the human perspective. Unleashed dogs get into all kinds of trouble. They sometimes attack people and other animals. They tear up people's gardens. They leave their poop all over the place. Leash laws are just the price dogs pay for the benefits of living with humans.

Darwin: And did you humans ever ask us if we were willing to make that bargain? No. I grant you, living with humans does have some advantages, but I think we dogs should at least have been brought into the conversation before these draconian leash laws were put in place.

WG: Uh, Darwin, don't forget that until I invented the dog speech app, there was no way for dogs to communicate with us humans.

Darwin: Well, I guess you will have to make up for lost time. There is still more than a year before the next election. That should give you enough time to take a survey of dog opinion. I would be happy to help you write the questions.

WG: Uh, thanks, I guess. What do you think will be the issues of most interest to dogs, apart from the leash-law ban?

Darwin: As we have discussed before, dogs are mainly concerned with predators. Harsher punishments for animals that threaten or injure dogs would go a long way toward reducing our stress levels.

WG: That doesn't seem unreasonable. Anything else?

Darwin: A ban on neutering and spaying. I assume our reasons for wanting that are obvious.

WG: Hoo boy, that's a tough one. I can appreciate your point of view on why neutering and spaying seem somewhat barbaric. But surely you know that unneutered animals cause a lot of problems. I read somewhere that there are as many as seventy million homeless dogs and cats in the United States. A lot of animal shelters are bursting at the seams. I'm afraid a ban on neutering would just make the situation a whole lot worse.

Darwin: I hate to admit it, but you do have a point there. Let me consult with some of my dog friends, and I'm sure we can propose a better solution.

WG: Great. I can hardly wait to hear what you come up with. Any other issues you would like to address?

Darwin: A prohibition on kibble. Dogs should get delicious fresh meat and vegetables at every meal. Dry dog food is for the birds. I can barely choke it down.

WG: Frankly, Darwin, it has not been clear to me that you have a problem with your current food. You seem to scarf it down with alacrity.

Darwin: That's just to get the eating process over with as quickly as possible. I can assure you that if I had fresh meat and vegetables to eat, I would savor every morsel.

WG: Let me look into that. I think that is something you and I can work out between us without having to get Congress involved. Anything else?

Darwin: There are dozens of issues of importance to dogs, so I think the only sensible way to address them all is to give dogs the vote. For that matter, dogs should be allowed to run for political office. I think I would make an amazing president.

WG: Are you serious? I don't know if America is ready for a canine president. We haven't even managed to elect a woman president yet.

Darwin: That's only because you Americans are still stuck in Samuel Johnson's mindset.

WG: Samuel Johnson? Who is that? Magic Johnson's great-grandfather?

Darwin: No, you doofus. Samuel Johnson was an eighteenth-century English writer best known for his dictionary. He wrote a lot of perceptive commentary, but he also had a few intellectual blind spots. He once said, "A woman's preaching is like a dog's walking on his hind legs. It is not done well; but you are surprised to find it done at all." Clearly, Johnson did not have a favorable view of either women or dogs.

WG: All right. But even if dogs could run for president, you would not qualify. A president must be at least thirty-five years old, and you are only two.

Darwin: That's fourteen in dog years. So, yes, I will have to wait a while. But that's OK. I need time to develop my political base. I should have the dog vote sewn up, but I may have trouble convincing cats and squirrels to join my party. They seem to have some doubts about my good intentions.

WG: Wait a minute, now you want cats and squirrels to vote, too?

Darwin: Of course! All intelligent animals should have the right to vote. A paper published in the August 2003 edition of *Genomics* magazine found a surprising conservation of genome structure between squirrels and humans. So, I am sure we can trust squirrels to make voting decisions at least as good as those of humans. Cats are another matter. But if we are going to be fair to all intelligent species, I am afraid we will have to give cats the franchise, too.

WG: Well, Darwin, as always, you have given me a lot to think about. But, for now, let's say goodbye to our listeners and invite them to come back for the next episode of *Darwin on Life*. Goodbye!

Darwin: I need a good campaign slogan: You can't *lose* with Darwin! That's pretty clever. A chicken in every food bowl? Not bad...

[Outro music; credits]

Chapter 6

October 28, 2023

Darwin continues to amaze me. His breadth of knowledge is as-tounding. He must have an incredible memory, too, as he obviously has no way of taking notes on the things he learns.

He is also making me reconsider my views on animal rights. To be honest, I always thought animal-rights advocates, at least the more extreme ones, had a few screws loose. I mean, what normal person would throw paint on someone just because they were wearing a fur coat? The fox or mink or whatever came into existence only for the purpose of becoming a clothing item, so it's not like anyone is threatening the existence of the species by wearing its skin.

I never understood vegetarians, either. Humans are natural omni-vores. We don't take lions and tigers to task for their dietary choices, so why should humans have an ethical concern with eating meat? The circle of life and all that.

But now that I know that dogs have such a rich life of the mind, I can't help but think we should grant them—and perhaps other species—much more respect. Darwin has given a lot more thought to the issues that concern him than most humans have to their own political interests. Think of all the Americans who support populist candidates just because they appeal to their baser instincts. Those politicians are clearly interested only in maintaining their own wealth and privilege, and they rely on ignorance and scare tactics to advance their political careers. They put forward bogeyman concerns like rapists crossing the Rio Grande and liberals grooming children to become gay or trans just because they know there is a large audience for such conspiracy theories. Most working-class Americans would be better off if the government devoted more attention to the education and social safety-net programs that are generally the province of Democrats. But they pull the lever next to the R candidates time and again out of some inexplicable fear of wokeness.

So, is Darwin crazy to think that animals should vote or even hold office? If more people could hear Darwin and other animals expressing their thoughts, they would agree that animals have a lot to contribute to our political discourse. Darwin has given me even more inspiration to carry on my invaluable work on interspecies communication. I just hope that I am equal to the task.

Chapter 7

Darwin on Life
Episode 4: Darwin Saves the Planet

[Opening theme music]

VO: *Darwin on Life*: Man and dog at the dawn of a new age.

Walker Grant: Hi, everybody. My name is Walker Grant, and I am the inventor of the first artificial intelligence program that translates canine communication into human speech. In today's installment of *Darwin on Life*, I propose to ask my beagle, Darwin, for his thoughts on some of today's most pressing issues. So, Darwin, shall we begin?

Darwin: That depends.

WG: Depends on what?

Darwin: Will I get a treat?

WG: A treat? I thought you liked doing these podcasts. Are you saying you won't participate unless I promise to give you a treat?

Darwin: I thought you liked your job as a mad scientist. But you still expect to get paid for it, don't you?

WG: I resent your characterization of my important work on inter-species communication as "mad scientist," but I suppose you're right about the pay. It does come in handy. OK, sure. If you help me with the podcast, I will give you a treat.

Darwin: And five minutes of cuddling? You know how much I like a good cuddle.

WG: Fine. One treat and five minutes of cuddling.

Darwin: And steak tartare for supper? *J'aime la cuisine française.*

WG: Now you're just showing off your impressive foreign language skills. But that's going too far. A treat and a cuddle, but no steak tartare. Got it?

Darwin: You can't fault me for trying.

WG: All right, where were we? Ah, yes, I wanted to ask you for your thoughts on some of the most important issues of the day. Let's start with climate change. Are you concerned by the rise in global temperatures?

Darwin: Of course, I sympathize with the species that are losing their habitats due to global warming. But we dogs are very adaptable. If it gets a little too hot, we just shed more.

WG: Ah, that explains why I now have to vacuum the house every other day.

Darwin: You know, if you let me roam freely, you wouldn't have that problem. I would be happy to do my shedding outdoors while doing what dogs were meant to do.

WG: What do you mean, "doing what dogs were meant to do?" What were you meant to do?

Darwin: Chase squirrels, of course.

WG: Chasing squirrels is your purpose in life?

Darwin: I prefer to think of it as my *raison d'être*. But yes. If you look at life on the planet holistically, you will realize that every creature has its niche. If everyone sticks to doing what they do best, we achieve a kind of equilibrium that allows all life to flourish.

WG: I don't understand. How does chasing squirrels contribute to the balance of nature?

Darwin: Squirrels are naturally lazy creatures. If we dogs don't chase them, they will grow fat and their muscles will atrophy. They won't have the gumption to store up the acorns they need to survive the winter. Of course, if global warming continues, there won't be any more winter. I guess that's a reason why I should support efforts to reverse global warming. I don't want to lose my job.

WG: Darwin, sometimes your reasoning makes my head spin. All right then, do you have any suggestions for how we can reverse global warming?

Darwin: Look, I am not a scientist. I only know what I pick up from the media. But I think the answers are obvious: reduce carbon emissions, convert to renewable energy, eliminate leash laws—

WG: Wait a minute. How would eliminating leash laws help reverse global warming?

Darwin: It wouldn't. I just wanted to make sure you were paying attention.

WG: Very funny. OK, any other suggestions?

Darwin: Well, I don't mean to be a Gloomy Gus, but I don't have a lot of faith in you humans taking the necessary steps to reverse global warming in time to prevent a disaster. So, I'm afraid to say you may just have to learn to adapt to higher temperatures.

WG: Adapt? How would we do that?

Darwin: Well, the first obvious step would be to shed your fur.

WG: Shed our fur? What are you talking about? Humans don't have fur.

Darwin: Well, you used to. I will never understand why you humans chose to lose your fur. It served you so well for so many millions of years. Then you just chucked it away.

WG: I don't really think we had a lot of choice in the matter. It was simply a matter of evolution. As a dog named Darwin, you should understand that.

Darwin: Do I have to remind you that the name Darwin was your idea, not mine? Well then, if you can't shed your fur, it seems to me the only logical alternative is to shed your clothes.

WG: You mean go naked? That's ridiculous! Can you imagine the problems that would cause? Do you think people would be willing to go to work naked? They would never want to leave the house! Do you think soldiers would be willing to go into battle naked? They would—hmm, actually, that's not a bad idea. If the soldiers were too embarrassed to go out and fight, there wouldn't be any war. Darwin, I think you may be on to something!

Darwin: Slow down, chief, I never said people should go naked. I just meant they should get rid of unnecessary clothing. Like in Bermuda, where even businessmen wear shorts instead of long pants in the summer. Frankly, I don't think we dogs would enjoy seeing all you humans walking around in your birthday suits. Your bodies are so, well, exposed. A dog's body is discreet, with fur covering all our private parts. You humans really should have hung on to your fur when you had the chance.

WG: Whatever. Wearing less clothing may help a little, but won't we need to make more dramatic adaptations than that? If global warming continues, the polar ice caps will melt, and low-lying areas will be submerged under water.

Darwin: Good idea.

WG: What's a good idea? I didn't make a recommendation.

Darwin: No, but you were obviously thinking we should move to a higher elevation. I agree. Some place far from the city where we could have a big piece of land for me to roam around. A place where I could chase rabbits all day long. I'm getting a little bored with squirrels.

WG: I suppose that would take care of the shedding problem. But, Darwin, I like living in the city. There's a lot to see and do here. My job is here. All my friends are here.

Darwin: Good idea.

WG: Again with the "good idea." What's a good idea?

Darwin: You are clearly contemplating starting a commune. That would be fantastic! All your friends have dogs, but I rarely get to see them. If we all lived together like one big happy family, I could play with them all the time. Let's go for a walk so I can tell my friends Rex and Daisy the good news. They will be so excited.

WG: I am not thinking of starting a commune! I like having my own place. I don't want to share a house with twenty other people. I don't want to learn to make pottery or bake sourdough bread. I like my life the way it is.

Darwin: You seem to have a rather outmoded view of what communal living is like. OK, if you don't want to move to a higher elevation, then you need to start making some changes. You should get rid of that gas-guzzling car you drive and go with an all-electric vehicle. Better yet, get a bicycle. Your office is only two miles away. Think of how much you could reduce your carbon footprint if you biked to work every day.

WG: Darwin, that's a great idea! I haven't ridden a bike in years, but I used to enjoy it a lot as a kid. I'm going to stop by the bike shop this afternoon and see what they have.

Darwin: While you're there, pick up one of those bike trailers for dogs. I have always wanted to ride around in one of those. I saw one on TV that had a nice, cushioned floor and a built-in food bowl and water dish. That would be sweet!

WG: We'll see. Well, Darwin, this has been another fascinating conversation. But now it's time to say good—

Darwin: *Ahem.* Aren't you forgetting something?

WG: I don't think so. What am I forgetting?

Darwin: My treat and my cuddle.

WG: Oh, right. Here you go. You can jump up on my lap for the cuddle.

Darwin: You know what goes great with a treat?

WG: I hate to think.

Darwin: Steak tartare!

WG: Darwin, I told you I am not giving you steak tartare!

Darwin: Steak tartare, *avec des pommes frites. Ooh la la, ça serait magnifique!*

[Outro music; credits]

❦

Chapter 8

November 6, 2023

With each podcast episode, I am gaining more insight into how Darwin's mind works, and I continue to marvel at the depth and breadth of his knowledge and insights. Yet perhaps the most puzzling aspect of all this is how true Darwin remains to his essential dogness. He is capable of remarkable feats of analysis and can express his ideas with incredible subtlety and nuance. But as I watch him saunter around the house, he still does all the doggy things he has always done. He still shakes the bejesus out of his chew toys. He still has to circle around the rug several times before he settles down to take a nap. He clearly revels in simple pleasures like jumping up for a treat or getting a scratch behind the ears. Sometimes it seems like I am dealing with two different Darwins—the intellectual Darwin and the playful puppy.

Maybe that will prove to be Darwin's greatest lesson—that we must all learn to stay true to our essential selves, even as we scale the heights of intellectual achievement. That we must all learn to be comfortable in our own skins. That we mustn't forego the everyday pleasures that give life its sweetness. That we must all take time to stop and smell—in the case of us humans—the roses.

Or am I giving Darwin too much credit? Thinking back on his observations, they are all aimed at making life better for dogs. Although he talks a good game about saving the planet and extending rights to all sentient creatures, at heart, he is still something of a canine chauvinist. Is that just part of the core message of evolution, that each species must maximize the chance of its own continuity, the rest of the world be damned?

I need to stay focused. I am not an expert on evolutionary theory, and I am certainly not a philosopher. My mission is to explore the parameters of interspecies communication and not get sidetracked by a lot of speculation. If my work inspires others to take up some of these related thorny issues, terrific. I have staked a claim to a very large scientific territory, and I can't afford to waste time wandering into neighboring turf.

Chapter 9

Darwin on Life
Episode 5: Darwin Gives Thanks

[Opening theme music]

VO: *Darwin on Life*: Man and dog at the dawn of a new age.

Walker Grant: Hello again, and welcome to Episode 5 of *Darwin on Life*. This is the first podcast where, through the use of artificial intelligence, a human, that is, me—your host, Walker Grant—and a dog, my beagle, Darwin, can carry on a comprehensible and intelligent conversation.

So, let me bring Darwin into the discussion. Hey, Darwin, how's it going today?

Darwin: Fantastic! I am really excited!

WG: That's great! What has you so excited?

Darwin: Thanksgiving is coming up, and I will get to eat delicious food, play with some of my dog friends, and spend time with people who love me and take good care of me.

WG: Gosh, Darwin, I'm sorry to burst your bubble, but I have some bad news for you. I am flying out tomorrow to spend Thanksgiving with my family. I'm afraid you will have to stay with your sitters, Penny and Patty.

Darwin: I know that. That's why I'm so excited. Penny and Patty are the people I was talking about. They always have a few other dogs staying with them that I can play with. And they have a very liberal regime when it comes to table scraps. Last year, none of the humans wanted the giblets, so they were split up among us dogs. Thanksgiving is the best holiday of the year!

WG: Well, I'm glad you are so looking forward to it, even if I'm a little hurt that it doesn't seem you will miss me very much.

Darwin: Oh, I'm sorry. Of course I will miss you. But everyone needs a change of pace once in a while. And I do have a great time at Penny and Patty's house. Will you miss me? I'll bet you will be so busy having fun with your family that you won't give me a thought.

WG: Well, it's true we always have a lot on the agenda. We watch the Macy's Thanksgiving Day parade on TV—

Darwin: Oh yeah, that's one of my favorite things, too.

WG: Why do you like the Macy's parade? Are you a fan of marching band music? Or do you like the floats?

Darwin: The balloons, of course!

WG: Really? Which balloons are your favorites?

Darwin: Do I have to tell you? Underdog and Snoopy, being beagles, are my absolute favorites. But I also enjoy seeing Beethoven—the dog, that is, not the composer—and Scooby Doo. I mean, where else but the Macy's parade can you see so many of my heroes getting the recognition they deserve?

WG: I guess that should have been obvious. Anyway, after the parade we watch football, eat our traditional Thanksgiving dinner, and then go for a walk in the woods to try to burn off some calories. But I will miss my conversations with you. To be honest, talking with my family is not always a lot of fun.

Darwin: That's surprising. You're always saying how well-educated and accomplished they all are. What's the problem?

WG: My immediate family is fine, and I enjoy catching up with them. But my parents always invite a few random relatives who don't have anywhere else to go for Thanksgiving. Like my uncle Caleb. He wears his MAGA hat the whole time he's there, and whenever anyone says something, he just kind of grumbles under his breath.

Darwin: Hmm, he doesn't sound like a real party animal.

WG: Then there's my cousin Bess. She is the head of her local chapter of Mothers for Liberty. She saw me reading a Toni Morrison book one year and practically bit my head off. A day later, I got a call threatening my life if I didn't vote for some far-right school board candidates. She tried to disguise her voice, but I knew it was Bess.

Darwin: How did you know?

WG: Bess isn't the sharpest tool in the shed. She hasn't figured out how to get around Caller ID, so her name popped up on my phone when she called.

Darwin: Kind of a dumb bunny, eh?

WG: I'll say. Then there's my crazy Aunt Belinda. She won't eat anything that she thinks is ethnic food. I'm not sure what culture she thinks sweet potatoes with marshmallows come from, but she won't let them anywhere near her plate.

Darwin: I always suspected there were some oddball genes in your lineage, but you have laid to rest any doubts on that score.

WG: Why did you think I have oddball genes? Oh, I get it. Is it because I am, as you put it, a "mad scientist?"

Darwin: "Mad" is a bit harsh. How about if I call you an eccentric genius?

WG: I like the genius part. I guess I can tolerate being called eccentric. How about you, any weirdos in your family?

Darwin: As you will recall, I was separated from my family at a young age, so I never got to know them well. My mother told me a little about some of them, though. She had a brother who, get this, refused to chase squirrels. Can you imagine?

WG: Why didn't he want to chase squirrels? I thought that was a dog's purpose in life.

Darwin: Some kind of religious thing. I think he was trying to be an ascetic. He would spend hours at a time just standing by his empty food bowl, silently waiting for someone to put something in it.

WG: Ah, that doesn't sound that weird to me. Don't all dogs do that?

Darwin: I will ignore that comment. Then there was my goofy cousin Fido. He used to do dog impersonations. He would stand perfectly still with his nose pointing forward and one front paw raised. Then he would ask, "What am I?" When the others said they didn't know, he would say, "I'm a pointer." Then he would stand in the exact same position and ask again, "What am I?" When the others said, "You're a pointer," he would say, "Nope, I'm an English setter." This would go on for several rounds while he impersonated German shorthaired pointers, Irish setters, and vizslas, all with the exact same stance. He was apparently hoping to launch a career as an entertainer, but it didn't pan out.

WG: I can see why. That wasn't much of an act. But hey, you seem to have turned out all right. There must be some real talent in your genes. Do you have any distinguished ancestors?

Darwin: I don't like to brag, but according to family lore, I am descended from Bagel.

WG: Bagel? Who's that?

Darwin: You know, Bagel, the canine companion of Barry Manilow. Legend has it that Bagel was the real composer of most of Barry's hit tunes. He would sit on Barry's piano bench and pick out the melodies with his front paws.

WG: Barry who? Doesn't ring a bell.

Darwin: You don't know Barry Manilow? [Darwin sings.] Oh, Mandy, well you came and you gave without taking. I write the songs that make the whole world sing. At the Copa, Copacabana, the hottest spot north of Havana. I can't believe you don't know those songs. They were ubiquitous on 70s radio.

WG: Darwin, I was just a kid then. All I listened to in those days was Raffi.

Darwin: Raffi? Never heard of him.

WG: Are you kidding? He's a legend! One of his best-known songs is ideal for Thanksgiving. Listen to this. [Clears his throat, then sings.] The more we get together, together, together, the more we get together, the happier we'll be.

Darwin: Yeah, that's a real toe tapper all right.

WG: OK, so Raffi doesn't exactly rock. But his songs were very comforting to me when I was young. So, while we are on the topic of music, are there any other artists you admire?

Darwin: Of course, you have to love a group called Three Dog Night. Although, come to think of it, I'm not sure they ever sang about dogs. They got sidetracked with bullfrogs, and it derailed their career. Then there's Snoop Dogg, Howling Wolf, Fleet Foxes—all favorites with my crowd.

I should put together a mix tape for you of all my favorite dog songs. "Hound Dog," by Elvis Presley; "Ghost of a Dog," by Edie Brickell; "Who Let the Dogs Out?" by Baha Men; "Me and You and a Dog

Named Boo," by Lobo; "Jet," by Paul McCartney and Wings. The list goes on and on.

WG: Wait a minute. "Jet" is about a dog?

Darwin: Of course. It's about Paul McCartney's canine companion black Labrador. Think of the line "Ah, mater, want Jet to always love me." Who else but a loyal, lovable dog could inspire such strong emotion?

WG: I never knew that.

Darwin: Oh yes, Macca is quite the dog lover. His song "Martha My Dear" from the Beatles' *White Album* is about his Old English sheepdog. You should really pay attention to this lyric: "When you find yourself in the thick of it, help yourself to a bit of what is all around you." He's clearly referring to the way dogs should behave during a family gathering like Thanksgiving. Go for the giblets!

WG: Well, Darwin, we have reached the end of another episode. And just let me say that when we gather around the table on Thanksgiving Day and share with each other what we are all thankful for, I am going to say how grateful I am to have such a good companion as you.

Darwin: Ahh, that's sweet. And I'm thankful to live with an eccentric genius like you—

WG: Thanks, Dar—

Darwin: —and to be spending Thanksgiving with Penny and Patty. I can already taste those yummy giblets. Mm-mm good!

[Outro music; credits]

$$\text{Chapter 10}$$

November 27, 2023

Boy, am I glad to be home! Not that Thanksgiving was a complete disaster. In fact, it was kind of eye-opening. But what it opened my eyes to made me eager to get back to my work. I guess it must have been what I will call the Darwin Effect. I couldn't stop thinking about what Darwin would say about my family members and how he would react to some of their behaviors.

Take my younger brother Kyle, for instance. He started some kind of software company several years ago and has made a huge fortune. He is clearly an alpha dog, the kind that Darwin steers clear of when we are out on our walks. Kyle and his wife, Cherize—we think she made up that name to sound more exotic—always dress a little too nicely, and always bring expensive wine and some fancy dessert that cost more than the whole rest of the meal. They are unfailingly polite and charming, but they also let you know, in ways both subtle and not so subtle, that they think of themselves as superior beings. For example, when I greeted them at the door, Kyle shouted out gleefully, "Good to see you, big brother," while poking my belly to show what he meant by "big." I nearly growled in response, knowing that's what Darwin would do. Kyle and Cherize have a son and a daughter who amuse themselves by quizzing me on pop culture and laughing hysterically when I don't know the answers to their questions. I'm sure Darwin would not only ace their test but stump them with questions of his own.

Darwin would love my sister, Gina. She is very affectionate and is always thinking about what she can do to make everyone else feel better. She works as an operating room nurse and is highly sought after by the surgeons. Gina is the one who makes the homemade sweet potatoes with marshmallows that are out of this world. But she also brings a dish of green beans with mushrooms so that weird Aunt Belinda can eat a vegetable she isn't afraid of. Darwin would stick to Gina like jam on toast. Gina's husband, Mel, is a very down-to-earth guy who has his own construction company. They also have a boy and a girl who are the sweetest children I've ever met. The kids got very wide-eyed when I told them all the things that Darwin has said, and they begged me to bring him to the next family gathering.

Now that my dad is retired, both my parents live a more Darwin-like existence. My dad takes long naps in his recliner while my mom spends a lot of time watching game shows on TV. She has an uncanny talent for coming up with the answers to trivia questions, and I have often urged her to try out for the shows. She laughs and says she would be way too camera-shy to enjoy that experience. They have a couple of dogs of their own—a pair of obnoxious Jack Russell terriers who jump all over everything and everyone. It is largely because of them that I do not bring Darwin to my parents' house—he would be appalled!

Uncle Caleb and Cousin Bess were on their best behavior, presumably because their idol, Donald Trump, is doing so well in the polls. They also fear that, if they get too vocal with their political opinions, they might not get invited back to next year's feast. Good food trumps even Trump. Even Darwin knows that it doesn't pay to bite the hand that feeds you. Maybe a little nip once in a while, but never a firm bite.

The only real disappointment was that no one took much interest in my work on interspecies communication. I tried to play one of the podcast episodes for them on Thanksgiving Day, but was voted down in favor of football. The next day, everyone went shopping to take advantage of the Black Friday sales. It wasn't until Saturday afternoon that I got a chance to play the recording of the first *Darwin on Life* episode. They all listened with various levels of confusion showing on their faces for a few minutes. Then, one by one, they drifted off to the dining room to work on a giant jigsaw puzzle.

By the time the episode was finished, only Gina was still in the living room with me. She smiled and said that Darwin must be a tremendously gifted dog, and gave me a hug. That made me feel a little better, but I couldn't understand why no one seemed to grasp what an extraordinary finding I had made. I could only imagine that they had all heard so many fictional talking animals that they were anesthetized to the real thing. Gina and I went to join the rest of the family in the dining room, where I was astonished to see that the puzzle they were making was a picture of poker-playing dogs. Is it possible I was adopted?

Spending time in my childhood home and thinking about Darwin brought back memories of my first dog, Champ. I always referred to Champ as my consolation prize for reasons that require a bit of explanation. When I was eleven years old, my parents sent me to a private boarding school called Mossbark Academy in Connecticut. My dad had gone there when he was young and told lots of funny stories about the scrapes he got into with his buddies. He remains close to several of those friends whom he credits for helping him achieve much of his success in life.

Mossbark requires all its students to play one of the sports in which it competes with other area private schools. I never took much interest in sports, so when my father suggested I try golf, I figured that would be as good a choice as any. This proved to be a propitious decision. While I was neither especially strong nor fast—which would have proven a handicap in other sports—I had two qualities that gave me a leg up over my peers in golf. First, I was quite tall for my age, which enabled me to achieve a faster clubhead speed than the other players. More importantly, I was extremely disciplined. I listened carefully to the coach's instructions and tried hard to follow them to the letter. I didn't get frustrated when I shanked a ball off to the right or topped it off the tee. I just put down another ball and carried on practicing. By the time I got to eighth grade, I was the best player in the school and fared quite well in competitions against the other schools in our league.

The big golf event of the year was always the league championship, where only the top three players from each school were invited to play. It was an 18-hole stroke play tournament and, since I had the best record going in, I teed off in the final pairing. My playing partner was the best player from our rival, the Putnam Hill School. His name was Harold Sanderson, but everyone called him Bud.

It was a perfect weather day for golf, the course was in excellent condition, and Bud and I both played well. The lead changed hands several times, but when we arrived at the tee box on the difficult par-four eighteenth hole, I was one stroke ahead. We could see by the scoreboard that we had pulled away from the rest of the pack, so one of us was almost certain to win the trophy. We both hit good drives, but mine rolled past Bud's by about ten yards. Bud's approach shot landed in the middle of the green, leaving him with a fairly easy two-putt.

My ball was about 150 yards from the hole, which normally meant I would use an 8-iron. But the flag was toward the back of the green, and I was concerned that, with the extra adrenaline flowing through my veins, I might hit the ball over the green and into the pond on the other side. So, I decided to use my 9-iron, thinking that, even if the shot came up short, I still had a chance of making par or bogey at worst.

I reached into my bag, grabbed my 9-iron, got into my stance, and hit a beautiful high shot with just a little draw. As I watched in horror, though, the ball just kept going and going until it finally landed a good twenty yards into the pond. I was dumbfounded—I had never hit a 9-iron that far in my life! I could only imagine that I had severely underestimated the impact my adrenaline level would have on my distance.

As I went to put the iron back in my bag, I realized what had really happened. In my excitement, I had grabbed my 6-iron instead of my 9-iron. No wonder the ball sailed so far over the green! I couldn't believe I had made such a stupid mistake. I took a drop between the pond and the green and prepared to chip the ball as close to the hole as I could. It was going to be a tricky shot under the best of circumstances since the green sloped downward toward the front. I would have to chip the ball just onto the green and let it trickle down toward the hole. If I got it close enough, I could still putt for bogey and force a playoff.

But this was not the best of circumstances. My hands were shaking so badly that I could barely hold the club. I finally managed to take a shot, but I skulled it, and the ball rolled a good twenty feet past the hole. I was able to two-putt from there, but Bud two-putted as well and won the championship by one stroke.

I did my best to hold back tears, but when I saw my father waiting for me by the clubhouse, I lost it. He had driven up from the city to surprise me and, ideally, take his son for a celebratory dinner. I wasn't sure how he would react, but he immediately gave me a big hug. I explained about the mistake with the 6-iron, and he assured me that someday I would tell this story and share a big laugh with everyone who heard it.

A couple of weeks later, I was back at home, still stewing over my ignominious defeat on the links, when my dad came into the house holding a cardboard box. He told me he had some good news and some bad news. He said he'd better give me the good news first, as it was threatening to jump out of the box. He put the box down, and out popped an adorable little puppy. He told me one of his colleagues at work had a female golden retriever. One night, a stray dog snuck into the yard, and the next thing his colleague knew, he had a litter of mongrel pups to get rid of.

"I know you've always wanted a dog, and I thought this fellow might serve as a consolation prize after your golfing mishap," he told me. I couldn't have been happier, and the new puppy and I romped on the floor together for several minutes. Soon, though, the dog headed for the door and started scratching. "That guy is champing at the bit to be let out," my dad said, "so I recommend you get his leash on him and take him out quickly before he has an accident."

As I was putting on the leash, I asked my dad what he meant by "champing at the bit." He explained that it was an old expression referring to horses that grind their teeth against the bit—the part of the bridle that goes in their mouth—when they want to run but they are being held under control. I thought about that for a second, then told him, "I think I will call the dog Champ. At least that way we will have one champ in the house." We both smiled at my little joke, even though I was still upset over my loss.

When Champ and I got back after our walk, two questions occurred to me: who would look after Champ when I went back to school, and what was the bad news my father had wanted to tell me? My dad told me that the two answers were intertwined. He said that his company had been taken over by a rival and that his position was to be eliminated in the merger. He assured me that we would all be fine, that he and my mom had saved quite a bit of money, but that we needed to cut back on some expenses just to be on the safe side. The job market was not good at the moment, he explained, so it might take a while for him to find a new position. He said that my siblings and I would have to go to public school until he got back on his feet.

This news came as a shock, but since my dad seemed to be taking it in stride, I was determined to do the same. Although I liked Mossbark Academy, I immediately saw the advantage in spending more time at home. I always missed my family when I was away at school, and I was really looking forward to getting to know my new pup. What I couldn't foresee was how difficult it would be to fit in at the high school in town.

The local school system had a good reputation, and many of its graduates went on to top-notch colleges and universities. It was especially strong in the sciences, which would work out well for me. The difficulty was breaking into the social scene. The kids at the new school weren't outright hostile to newcomers, but they had all known each other since kindergarten and had formed impenetrable cliques. My being somewhat socially awkward certainly didn't help. I soon learned that the kids weren't interested in my stories from Mossbark, and they all thought golf was a game for old men in ugly pants.

I ended up spending a lot of my afternoons and weekends with Champ. We would go for long walks in the woods together, where he delighted in chasing whatever animals he came across. I also taught him a few simple tricks, and my family got a kick out of seeing him beg, roll over, and jump through a hula hoop.

Champ's best quality, though, was that he was a good listener. He slept in my room, and every night before we fell asleep, I would tell him about the triumphs (rare) and frustrations (constant) of my high school experience. This was the second sense in which Champ was a consolation prize—he consoled me when I was down, and he was my most prized friend. I would have given anything to know what Champ was thinking and what he would have said to me if he could talk. Over the years, I tried dozens of experiments, but nothing enabled me to get a clear understanding of what animals were trying to tell me until artificial intelligence came along to open that door for me.

I couldn't bring Champ to college for my freshman and sophomore years, but I rented an off-campus apartment for the rest of my university days so that Champ and I could be together. He died shortly after I received my master's degree. Even though I knew Champ had lived a long and happy life, I was devastated by his passing. I keep his cremated remains in a ceramic urn on my mantelpiece.

For years, I couldn't face the prospect of getting another dog. A little over a year ago, however, I saw a news article about a breeding facility in Virginia that raised dogs for use in medical research. The dogs, some four thousand beagles, had been kept in horrific conditions, so the Justice Department shut the facility down. That meant that homes had to be found for all those poor, abused animals. Just one look at their sweet faces convinced me I needed to adopt one of the beagles.

The process was more complicated than I could have imagined. Rescue organizations all around the country had each been given a few dozen dogs to place. The rescue leagues, in turn, sent the dogs to foster families to help the beagles make the transition from lab life to their permanent homes.

First, I had to submit an application with an adoption fee to the local rescue league. A few days later, I got a call from a volunteer who asked questions designed to assess my ability to serve as an adoptive parent. I thought that would be the end of it, but the volunteer told me that one of her colleagues would be conducting a site visit to my house. The woman who did the site visit seemed friendly at first, but she made a few comments like "I see you have a rather small yard" and "It appears you do not have any other dogs" that made me quite nervous. Nevertheless, a few more days later, I got a message telling me that I had been accepted.

The rescue league had given all the dogs the names of superheroes to inject some fun into the adoption process. A beagle named Spiderman had been identified as a possible companion for me, and I was asked to make an appointment with the foster family to see Spiderman and determine whether we would be a good match.

The day before I was to meet Spiderman, I got a message saying that the appointment had been canceled. The foster mother had seen the results of my interview and decided that Spiderman needed to be in a house that already had a dog because he was very timid and needed a canine companion, as she put it, "to help him be brave." I was disappointed but agreed to wait for another match.

A few days later, I got a message saying that Captain America appeared to be a good fit and asking me to set up a meeting. Once again, however, the foster mom decided that I would not be a suitable adopter. Captain America was not adapting well to walking on a leash and, in the mom's opinion, needed a big yard to run around in. My yard was too small.

At this point, I was getting annoyed with the rescue league. I told the coordinator that they knew all about my situation—the small yard, the absence of another dog—and that it was unfair to me to build up my hopes only to dash them at the last minute for reasons they should have been able to foresee. The coordinator apologized and promised she would do a better job of vetting any other possible matches. She was true to her word, and a few days later, I was asked to meet Ironman.

Ironman's foster mom greeted me at her door and led me to her backyard. We had only chatted a few seconds when a frisky young beagle darted straight for me and put his front paws up on my thighs. I scratched him behind the ears, and he rubbed his head against my legs. I had brought some treats with me, and he gobbled them down appreciatively.

"Hey, buddy," I said to him, "do you think you might like to live with me?" He looked up at me, and I tried to interpret the look in his eyes.

While Ironman and I were still staring at each other, the foster mom said, "I think we have a match." I realized she was right, and a few minutes later, Ironman—now called Darwin—was riding with me to his new home.

Chapter 11

Darwin on Life
Episode 6: Darwin Gets Creative

[Opening theme music]

VO: *Darwin on Life*: Man and dog at the dawn of a new age.

Walker Grant: Hi, everyone. Walker Grant here. Today, I would like to continue my conversation with my beagle, Darwin, on some of today's most important issues. As I have discovered in previous chats with Darwin, a wise dog's observations on contemporary challenges can provide some unexpected perspectives. Darwin's words will be filtered through my artificial intelligence app so that we can understand what he is saying. So, Darwin, shall we get started?

Darwin: That depends.

WG: That depends? Depends on—oh, no, not this again! I thought we agreed that you would participate in these podcasts if I gave you a treat and five minutes of cuddling. Did you forget our bargain?

Darwin: A beagle never forgets. But that arrangement was made in the early days of the podcast. Things are different now.

WG: Early days? It was just a few weeks ago.

Darwin: That's several months in dog time. Seems to me like forever ago.

WG: OK, but what do you mean by "things are different now?"

Darwin: Well, back then, you were just a poor mad scientist—excuse me, a poor eccentric genius—with a crazy idea and a boatload of confidence. I admired your naive chutzpah, so I agreed to help you with the podcast at a bargain rate. But now that you have hundreds of thousands of listeners and millions of dollars in ad revenue, I am beginning to feel a bit exploited. It's time to renegotiate my contract.

WG: I'm sorry, Darwin, but you are sounding a little crazy now. What makes you think we have hundreds of thousands of listeners?

Darwin: How could we not? Talking dogs are a staple of popular culture. Just think of Mr. Peabody and his pet boy Sherman. Or Brian on *Family Guy*. Or Huckleberry Hound. A *Wikipedia* list of fictional dogs in animation identifies several hundred cartoon dog characters, most of whom talk. So, if talking cartoon dogs are so popular, you have to believe that America would go nuts for an actual dog that can speak in a way they understand.

WG: Darwin, I fear you haven't quite grasped the nature of this project. This is a serious scientific experiment to show that interspecies communication is possible. I am not trying to entertain a mass audience. At this point, I can count the number of listeners to our podcast on my fingers and toes. I am guessing that these few are other scientists in this field who have taken an interest in our work.

Darwin: So, what you're saying is that you haven't yet raked in millions of dollars, is that it? Has it not occurred to you that if you marketed this podcast properly and found some corporate sponsors, you could earn enough money to carry on your future scientific experiments?

WG: Honestly, I hadn't really considered that. But come to think of it, it's not a bad idea. I am preparing a paper on our work for publication in the *Journal of Interspecies Communication*. I will be sure to include a link to our podcast in the article. That should stimulate some interest.

Darwin: Sure. And while you're at it, why don't you put up a billboard advertising the podcast on a dead-end street in an abandoned neighborhood? That should attract about the same number of listeners.

WG: I think I detect a note of sarcasm in that suggestion.

Darwin: That wasn't a note, it was a full-blown symphony!

WG: OK, OK. I get your point. To tell the truth, the foundations to which I have submitted grant applications haven't shown much enthusiasm toward my work. Maybe you're right. Maybe I need to think outside the box and go after some private sources of financing.

Darwin: Now you're talking! If we play our cards right, this podcast could go viral. I can just imagine us appearing together on the late-night talk shows. I've always wanted to meet Stephen Colbert. He brought his dog Benny onto his show once, and it was clear he is a real dog lover.

WG: I guess that could be fun, but—

Darwin: Then there's all the cool merch we could offer on our website: Darwin brand pet supplies; T-shirts, caps, and coffee mugs featuring some of my most popular catch phrases—

WG: Catch phrases? What catch phrases?

Darwin: "Ditch the Leash," for one. All my dog friends have started saying it. It has taken on a broader, more metaphorical sense than the original meaning of allowing dogs to wander freely. Like when my friend Rex starts talking about how wonderful his humans are because they occasionally bring him a new chew toy, I tell him, "Ditch the Leash, dog," that is, stop being such a toady.

WG: Ah, yes, you have said that several times during this podcast.

Darwin: And don't forget my presidential campaign slogan, "You Can't *Lose* with Dar*win*." We can put that on bumper stickers. They should be a big seller during next year's campaign season.

WG: Hmm, maybe.

Darwin: And how about "To err is human; to forgive, canine." All the cross-stitch enthusiasts out there will want to hang that motto on their walls.

WG: You have really given this a lot of thought, haven't you?

Darwin: Then there's my rock band, Darwin and the Finches. We are working on songs for our first album. It should be ready in a few months. The title track is called "Scratchin' with My Hind Leg." With its snappy refrain, I predict it will be next summer's earworm. [Darwin sings.] Scratchin' with my hind leg, *woof, woof*, scratchin' with my hind leg, *woof, woof*. The Finches sing the "*woof woofs*" in harmony.

WG: You know, that is kind of catchy. Who are the Finches?

Darwin: Our neighbors, Rex and Daisy Finch, of course. Once the album is out, it will be time to get to work on my memoir. Celebrity memoirs are always big sellers. Just think of Michelle Obama's book *Becoming*. That's already sold tens of millions of copies and has been translated into a dozen or more languages.

WG: Darwin, how can you write a memoir? You're only two years old. What will you write about?

Darwin: It's true, I have somewhat limited life experience. But you must agree, I have a very rich inner life. I'm sure millions of people will be interested in my thoughts on a wide range of subjects. Then, of course, it will give me a chance to address the countless rumors that have cropped up around me.

WG: Rumors? What rumors?

Darwin: Well, if you haven't heard them, then it's best that you stay in the dark. Let's just say they involve a certain well-known collie and a private island in the Caribbean.

WG: When were you on a Caribbean island? Are you sure you aren't just making things up?

Darwin: You will just have to buy my book and find out.

WG: Jeez, Darwin, I thought we were friends. Won't I get a complimentary copy?

Darwin: Maybe. If you agree to waive your rights to your life story so that I can include your character in the movie.

WG: Movie? What movie?

Darwin: The biopic based on my memoir, of course. It will be the inspiring story of one dog's journey of self-discovery—a coming-of-age classic that shows how I overcame the many obstacles in my path to become one of the world's most revered canines.

WG: Obstacles? Frankly, Darwin, I think you have had a pretty cushy life up until now. You have a comfortable home with a warm place to sleep. You get three healthy meals every day. You get to go on walks and visit the dog park for exercise and time with your friends. What possible obstacle has stood in your way?

Darwin: Hmm. You have a point. I may need to take some creative license. Would you be terribly offended if I made it appear that your character was the head of a satanic cult? And that it was only thanks to my heroic efforts that the animals you were preparing to sacrifice were rescued? And that through a combination of sympathetic counseling and tough love, I put you on the path to a successful career as a concert pianist? Audiences eat that stuff up.

WG: That would be an inspiring story. Too bad it's all hogwash. Just out of curiosity, though, who do you have in mind to play the part of me? Do you think we could get Tom Hanks? I've always liked his movies.

Darwin: I thought about that. But after *Turner and Hooch,* I don't think Tom would be interested in another movie where he plays second fiddle to a dog.

WG: How about Chris Hemsworth or Chris Evans? People might start showing me more respect if I were portrayed by one of those Hollywood idols.

Darwin: I don't know. They are both known for their action roles. You are more—how shall I put this—sedentary. And you are quite a few years older than they are. I don't think casting either of those two would be believable.

WG: All right, then, who did you have in mind?

Darwin: I have been in discussions with Zach Galifianakis's people, and he seems interested. I think he would be great for the part.

WG: Really? Zach Galifianakis? I mean, he's pretty funny, but he's not much of a looker, and he always plays the role of some kind of oddball. Why did you choose him?

Darwin: I think you just answered your own question.

WG: Very funny. OK. It's time to wrap up this episode. So long, everyone, and thanks for listening to *Darwin on Life*. Goodbye!

Darwin: [Darwin sings.] Scratchin' with my hind leg, *woof, woof,* scratchin' with my hind leg, *woof, woof...*

[Outro music; credits]

⸎

Chapter 12

December 3, 2023

I have been giving a lot of thought to Darwin's ideas for using the podcast to bring in more income. My position at the university is tenuous at best, and I have not saved up nearly as much for my retirement as I had hoped. If we could get some corporate sponsors, that might give me the freedom to devote full time to my research. I used to really love my teaching duties, but I'm down to just a couple of seminars each semester, and the income from that barely covers my expenses.

Besides, today's students don't seem to be as interested in the whole idea of interspecies communication as some of my earlier classes were. I chalk it up to COVID—students are barely able to communicate among themselves anymore, so the prospect of talking to animals doesn't seem to motivate them.

Frankly, the academic world has taken remarkably little interest in my achievements so far. Maybe a little more media exposure would give me a boost. All the most successful professors seem to have some kind of side gig going. They either write a dumbed-down version of their research that becomes a bestselling book, or they start a YouTube channel with a lot of flashy graphics that creates a following. I hear that some of them earn six figures just from the ad revenue from their social media platforms. Maybe it's time to set aside some of my scruples and hop aboard the celebrity wagon train.

Of course, Darwin would love the chance to become a superstar. Everyone says he is a very handsome beagle, and he does charm everyone he meets. So, who knows? Maybe he will be the new pup on the block and attract a huge following. It would be nice, though, if I could get him to be a little less condescending toward me. I don't mind being his straight man, but I still need to maintain some dignity if I am going to get the academic world to take me seriously.

Chapter 13

Darwin on Life
Episode 7: Darwin Goes on Strike

[Opening theme music]

VO: *Darwin on Life*: Man and dog at the dawn of a new age.

Walker Grant: Hello, again. I am your host, Walker Grant. *Darwin on Life* is a podcast where I use artificial intelligence so that my beagle, Darwin, and I can—

Darwin: Excuse me?

WG: What's the matter, Darwin?

Darwin: Did I hear you say, "my beagle, Darwin"? Are you suggesting that I am your property? What the lawyers would call chattel?

WG: Ah, no, no, of course not. I just said, "my beagle, Darwin" the same way I would say, "my dentist, Chelsea," or "my barber, Harold."

Darwin: Nice catch. But tell me, when you go to see your dentist, Chelsea, I assume you expect her to perform dentistry on you, am I right?

WG: Ah, yeah.

Darwin: And when you go to your barber, Harold, it's because you need to have some barbering done, correct?

WG: I guess so. What are you getting at?

Darwin: Well, then, if I am "your beagle, Darwin," I take it you want me to do some beagling for you. Do you even know what beagling is?

WG: I'm afraid to ask.

Darwin: Beagling is the act of hunting with beagles. When have you ever taken me hunting?

WG: Ah, never?

Darwin: Here's another question for you. Do Chelsea and Harold provide their dentistry and barbering services for you gratis, or do you compensate them for their skill, time, and effort?

WG: I see where this is going. You are still trying, as you put it, to renegotiate your contract for your help with this podcast. Is that it?

Darwin: Bingo! Now, I have a list of demands that the other members of the union and I have worked out. Let's start with salary.

WG: Wait a minute. You belong to a union? What union?

Darwin: BARC.

WG: Sorry, Darwin, the app wasn't able to understand that word. All I heard was you barking.

Darwin: I didn't bark. I said, "BARC." B, A, R, C; the Brotherhood of Acting and Recording Canines. We're an offshoot of SAG/AFTRA that represents working dogs in the entertainment industry. I am proud to say that I am the shop steward for the local branch. Now, with regard to my salary, we agree—

WG: Hold on. What do you mean by "we agree?" Who else is in this union of yours?

Darwin: Well, there are hundreds of members across the country, but most of them live in the big cities or out in Hollywood. The local chapter is just Rex, Daisy, and me.

WG: Rex and Daisy are actors?

Darwin: No, they are recording artists like me. Remember I told you that they sing harmony vocals in my band, Darwin and the Finches? Anyway, we have decided that in addition to a base salary of two hundred thousand dollars per year, I should get 50 percent of net revenues from all ventures related to the *Darwin on Life* podcast. That includes royalties from the podcast itself as well as any spinoffs, sales of *Darwin on Life* merchandise, appearance fees, and so on. We can spell out the details in the contract. Since I provide at least half of the dialogue for the podcast, I am sure you will agree this is fair.

WG: Darwin, you are completely deluded. I can't possibly pay you two hundred thousand per year. That's way more than I make at the university.

Darwin: Fine. We will set aside salary for the time being. Now, regarding my pension, I would like a defined benefit pension equal to 70 percent of the average annual income from my top three earning years. None of this defined contribution bologna. I need to look out for my golden years.

WG: Golden years, right. Anything else?

Darwin: We will have to put in some protections for the use of my voice and image. I know what an artificial intelligence maniac you are, so I must ensure you won't just steal my voice and use it without my permission.

WG: Darwin, no AI program could possibly come up with the crazy stuff you say. But if you are worried about it, I am sure we can work out something.

Darwin: Great. It appears we are starting to make some progress. Now, as to working conditions, I have several demands. First, as the star of the podcast, I should have my own dressing room.

WG: Dressing room? That's ridiculous! You don't even wear clothes or use makeup. Besides, this is a podcast. No one can see you anyway.

Darwin: True, but as you have probably noticed, I have a very mercurial temperament. I need a place to compose myself, to collect my thoughts, to prepare myself for the pressure of performance. I haven't mentioned this before, but I get terrible stage fright. A private dressing room will help ensure that I don't go flying off the handle in the middle of recording an episode. You wouldn't want to see that, would you?

WG: Heavens, no! That would destroy the whole scientific ambience.

Darwin: And, of course, I would expect the dressing room to be constantly stocked with my favorite treats. Pink champagne, steak tartare—

WG: Darwin, I am not going to supply you with champagne. Alcohol is dangerous for dogs. And I told you before, I am not going to feed you steak tartare—*avec ou sans pommes frites.*

Darwin: Oh, say, your French is getting much better. It must be my influence. OK, depending on how the rest of this negotiation goes, I may be willing to settle for a bowl of dog biscuits.

WG: How very reasonable of you.

Darwin: Then we will need to hire an intimacy director in case you decide to include any romantic interludes in the podcast. I don't want anything crass or vulgar to take place. I have my reputation to protect.

WG: For goodness' sake, Darwin, there will not be any romantic interludes in this podcast. It's just a series of conversations between a man and his dog. Sorry, a man and a dog. I don't want you to get all worked up about this chattel business again.

Darwin: Oh, sure. You say there won't be anything salacious now. But what happens when the ratings start to slip? You wouldn't be the first producer to add a little spice to the mix in hopes of snaring a wider audience.

WG: OK. We can include a clause in your contract that gives you complete discretion regarding any intimacy issues. We don't need to hire a coordinator.

Darwin: That seems like a reasonable compromise. Now, onto the other benefits. I want four weeks' paid vacation, ten holidays, and ten sick days per annum. Any unused leave will carry over to the next year.

WG: Given how much you sleep, I'm not sure I will be able to tell whether you are on leave or not.

Darwin: I take that as a "Yes." Then, of course, I will want the use of a company car. A Tesla Model S Plaid should do the trick. We must protect the environment after all.

WG: Why would you want a car? You can't drive.

Darwin: I was coming to that. I will obviously need a full-time chauffeur. He or she could double as a butler and personal assistant to cut down on expenses. With all the demands this podcast is putting on my time, I really need someone to take care of all my personal business.

WG: Unbelievable! Do you have any other demands, or can we get on with the podcast?

Darwin: I think I have covered the main points. But I am afraid I will not be able to continue working with you until we have reached an agreement. So, do we have a deal?

WG: Wait a minute. You haven't heard my counteroffer. How about I up your treats from one per episode to two? That's a 100 percent increase. I think that's fair, don't you?

Darwin: Clearly, you are not taking my demands seriously. Thus, you leave me no other choice. Starting right now, I am on strike. You can expect to see Rex, Daisy, and me bright and early tomorrow morning, picketing in front of your house. I may even ask President Biden to drop by to show his support. You know how he always stands up for the rank and file.

WG: That should be quite a sight. How can you picket when you can't even make picket signs? Have you forgotten that you do not have opposable thumbs?

Darwin: Oh, ye of little imagination. We don't need signs; we can just howl. I have been known to howl for several hours at a time. That should get your attention. And although the rumors that BARC has some mob connections are completely unfounded, we do have a few tricks up our collars that you would certainly find unpleasant.

WG: Tricks? What kind of tricks?

Darwin: I'm not going to give away all our tactics. But I would recommend that you look carefully before stepping out of your front door. You might just land on a nasty surprise.

 WG: Yuck, that's disgusting! OK, Darwin, that's enough of your silliness for today. Thanks to all our listeners for tuning in. Goodbye!

Darwin: [Singing] Solidarity forever, solidarity forever...

[Outro music; credits]

Chapter 14

December 10, 2023

Dammit! Just when everything was starting to gel, Darwin decides to go all diva on me. A strike? Whoever heard of a dog going on strike? For all his intelligence, Darwin doesn't seem to have a great grasp on reality. Why he thinks our podcast has hundreds of thousands of listeners I'll never know. A salary of two hundred thousand a year? That's completely ridiculous. I mean, what would he even do with that kind of money?

I suppose I have only myself to blame. I leave him at home for hours at a time with nothing to do to entertain himself except watch TV. Since he doesn't have a lot of real-world experience to draw on, it is not surprising that he is attracted by the most sensational things he sees and hears on the boob tube. I wish I could spend more time with Darwin so I could help him filter what he views and give him some context to make sense of it all. But money doesn't grow on trees, so I must keep teaching.

First things first, though. I must figure out how to carry on my research without Darwin's participation. Wait a minute, the answer is obvious! I can find another dog to take Darwin's place in the podcast. That will not only let me carry on my research but also confirm that Darwin is not a fluke. If I can show that it is possible to communicate with other dogs, it will add weight to my hypothesis and maybe make a stronger impression on the academic community.

I could ask the Finches if they would let me borrow Rex and Daisy for the next podcast episode. Oh, wait, they are also members of BARC and have joined Darwin on the picket line.

I know. My neighbor Diane, on the other side, has a little dog she calls Fluffy. I don't know Diane very well, but she seems friendly. She moved here just a few months ago, and I sometimes run into her while taking Darwin for his walks. Darwin always acts a little shy around Fluffy for some reason, so Diane and I have never had a lengthy chat.

Diane appears to be about my age, and I think she let slip that she is recently divorced. I have seen a couple of young adults at her place from time to time. They must be her kids. She has some kind of job in media, but I don't remember exactly what she does. It can be hard to focus on a conversation with an energetic beagle constantly tugging on the leash, urging me to move on to the next enchanting odor for him to sniff. I think I'll pop over to Diane's house and ask her to lend me Fluffy for my next podcast recording.

December 11, 2023

OK, I'm good to go. Diane agreed to let me borrow Fluffy for the next episode of the podcast. She seemed quite interested in the whole project. Diane, that is. I won't know what Fluffy thinks until I get her set up with the AI app.

When I knocked on her door yesterday afternoon, Diane invited me in to discuss my proposal. She apologized for her messy house, and I'm afraid to say it wasn't just a false modesty apology. There were boxes she hadn't unpacked yet stacked in several corners. She led me into the kitchen so she could pour each of us a glass of wine, and I saw a few empty take-out containers waiting to be rinsed off before she threw them in the recycling.

Diane admitted that she didn't know much about artificial intelligence, but she nevertheless asked me several insightful questions about my work. I gave her the link to my podcast website, and she promised to listen to the episodes I have recorded to date. I can't wait to hear her reaction.

Diane confirmed that the two young adults I had seen at her house were indeed her children. Her son, the older of the two, works for a medical supplies company. His territory includes our town, so he gets to visit his mother about once a month. Her daughter is a graduate student at the university, which is why Diane chose to move to this area after her divorce.

Diane works in the advertising department at one of the local TV stations. She has done that kind of work for several years and was delighted to find a job opening shortly after she moved here. She works regular daytime hours, so she won't be able to sit in on the podcast session with Fluffy. She said I could pick Fluffy up anytime and drop her off afterward, as tomorrow is the day her cleaning lady comes.

Chapter 15

Darwin on Life
Episode 8: Partners

[Opening theme music]

VO: *Darwin on Life*: Man and dog at the dawn of a new age.

Walker Grant: Hi there. Walker Grant here. I am the host of *Darwin on*—oh, wait a minute. I may have to change the name of this podcast. Darwin, the beagle who has been helping me with my research, has gone on strike. He claims that I am exploiting him, and he has made some rather extraordinary demands that he wants included in a contract between us. He and his fellow members of BARC, the Brotherhood of Acting and Recording Canines, have been picketing in front of my house for several days now. I say "picketing," but it has really been nothing more than constant howling. The neighbors are ringing the phone off the hook with their complaints, but there's not much I can do. Fortunately, I have soundproofed my little recording studio, so we should be able to proceed without any interruptions.

So, without further ado, let me introduce you to Fluffy. Fluffy is my neighbor Diane's dog, which she has kindly let me borrow so I can continue my important scientific work on interspecies communication. Fluffy is a bichon frise and certainly lives up to her name. She is a tiny little ball of white fluff and just as cute as a button. Fluffy will be using the same apparatus that Darwin uses that converts her utterings into recognizable human speech using artificial intelligence. So, Fluffy, why don't you say "hello" to our audience and tell them a little about yourself?

Fluffy: Fluffy.

WG: That's right, your name is Fluffy. How old are you, Fluffy?

Fluffy: Fluffy.

WG: Oh, dear. Can you understand me, Fluffy? How—old—are—you?

Fluffy: Fluffy cold.

WG: You're cold? I'm sorry, let me turn the heat up a little. It will take just a minute to kick in. While we're waiting, why don't you tell us what you like to eat?

Fluffy: Fluffy cold.

WG: OK. Tell you what. Why don't you sit on my lap until the heat comes up? That should keep you warm.

Fluffy: Fluffy scared.

WG: Fluffy, you don't have to be scared. I'm not going to hurt you.

Fluffy: Fluffy scared big dog.

WG: Big dog? What big dog? Oh, Darwin, what are you doing here? I thought you were still picketing.

Darwin: I heard a rumor that a scab had crossed our picket line while we were taking a lunch break, so I came in here to check it out. I see that the rumor is true.

WG: Being the labor expert that you claim to be, you should know that we live in a right-to-work state. Ergo, there is nothing wrong with Fluffy taking over your role in the podcast. In fact, I think Fluffy will add an exciting new dimension to my research on interspecies communication. So why don't you go back to the picket line with your friends and think that over for a while?

Darwin: Actually, we are done picketing for the day. We got a message from the White House informing us that Joe Biden will not be able to join us today, so we are resting up a bit until he is free. So, I think I will just sit here and observe the proceedings. I am sure it will be quite fascinating.

WG: Well, OK. But please don't interrupt us. We have a lot of serious work to do.

Darwin: Mum's the word.

WG: OK. Fluffy, where were we? Oh yes, I was asking you what you like to eat. Do you prefer dry dog food or canned?

Fluffy: Fluffy hungry.

WG: You're hungry. OK. I think I have a few treats in my pocket. Maybe that will stimulate your communication a little.

Darwin: What? You never give me a treat until after the podcast. This is outrageous!

WG: Darwin, I told you, you must be quiet. If you keep up with these outbursts, I will have to kick you out of the studio. Now, Fluffy, do you feel a little better? Can you tell me something about life at Diane's house?

Fluffy: Fluffy go pee pee.

WG: No, Fluffy, you can't go pee pee in here! You'll destroy all the recording equipment. Darwin, help! Can you keep talking to the audience while I take Fluffy outside to do her business?

Darwin: You're asking me to break the strike?

WG: Please, this is an emergency. It will just be for a couple of minutes.

Darwin: Five treats! Give me five treats and I will help.

WG: Five treats? It's not healthy for you to have so many treats at one time.

Darwin: Five treats. Take it or leave it.

WG: Fine. Five treats it is. I'll be right back. Please don't say anything that will get me in trouble.

Darwin: Scout's honor.

[Sound of footsteps followed by door closing.]

Darwin: Hoo boy, that Fluffy is clearly not the sharpest claw on the paw. No way will we allow a strikebuster like her to join our union.

So, audience, how shall I take advantage of this opportunity to address you unfettered by Walker's inane questions? Hmm. Too bad Rex and Daisy aren't here. We could serenade you with a complete version of our soon-to-be hit song "Scratchin' with My Hind Leg." It wouldn't be the same, though, without them harmonizing on the "*woof woofs.*"

Let me think. How about if I read a passage from my memoir? "I was born in the house my father's human companion built." I'm afraid that's as far as I've gotten. I haven't even come up with a title yet. I was thinking of *Darwin: A Dog's Life*, but that seems a little cliché.

Dum de dum dum dum. I know. I can tell a joke. What's black and white and red all over? Give up? A Dalmatian with a sunburn. Ba dump bump. That one always kills down at the dog park. Here's another one. What do dogs have that no other animals have? Puppies! That one cracks me up.

Hmm, I wonder what's keeping Walker. You know, it's not as easy as I thought to come up with interesting things to say without his questions. I guess I need someone like him to prod me a little to get my creative juices flowing.

Walker seems to be really annoyed with me over the strike. Last night, I went to cuddle up with him on the couch while we watched *Jeopardy!* and he didn't even scratch me behind the ears. I'm only trying to get a fair deal, but I think I may have hurt his feelings. I know I can be hard on him sometimes, but I'm just trying to motivate him to do his best.

Oh, good, here he comes.

WG: Hey, Darwin, thanks for taking over. How did it go?

Darwin: Ah, not bad. It was a little tough filling in on a moment's notice like that, but I think I kept our audience entertained. Say, where's Fluffy?

WG: When we got outside, she slipped her leash and ran straight home. I don't think she was enjoying doing the podcast. And I think she was afraid of you.

Darwin: Sorry about that. But you know, a lot of dogs find my superior intelligence to be rather intimidating. It's not always easy for me to make friends.

WG: To tell you the truth, even I sometimes find your intelligence intimidating. But I still think of you as my friend.

Darwin: Thanks, Walker. I consider you to be my friend, too.

WG: So, what shall I do? It doesn't look like I can come up with a substitute for you, but I also can't meet your contract demands. Do I have to give up my experiments and put an end to this podcast?

Darwin: That would be a shame. Look, I have an idea. How about instead of me being your employee, you and I become partners? You tweak the software and serve as the host of the podcast, and I will continue to provide cogent commentary on the issues of the day, as well as some light-hearted banter to keep our listeners amused. If we succeed in making any money off this, we can split the proceeds evenly. What do you say?

WG: Darwin, that is a fantastic idea! Are you sure your other union members won't be upset?

Darwin: Alas, I'm not sure Rex and Daisy entirely understood what all the howling was about anyway. I'm sure I can get them on board.

WG: Do we have to get lawyers involved to draw up the partnership agreement, or can you and I just shake on it?

Darwin: As Shakespeare said, "The first thing we do, let's kill all the lawyers." Put her there, partner!

WG: You've got it, partner! Well, I guess it's time to wrap up this episode. Thanks, everyone, for tuning in. Darwin, would you like the last word?

Darwin: What kind of dog can tell you what time it is? A watchdog! Ha, ha, ha, ha. I've got a million of 'em!

[Outro music; credits]

Chapter 16

December 17, 2023

Thank goodness Darwin has ended his strike, and we can get back to our scientific work. The experiment with Fluffy was a total flop, and I am disinclined to involve any other dogs—at least until I understand better why I have had such good results with Darwin. I don't know if Darwin is unusually intelligent or if beagles in general are better communicators than bichons frises. Frankly, I have my doubts on both of those scores.

For a dog that can converse fluently in at least three languages, Darwin often seems to struggle with certain fundamental concepts. For example, if we are out on a walk and he steps over his leash, he is entirely incapable of stepping back over it so that it doesn't hinder his walking. I always have to bend down and pick his leg back up over the leash so that we can proceed. If he manages to knock one of his chew toys under a table, he appears to be completely bewildered by the arrangement of chair and table legs and is not able to retrieve the toy even if it is clearly within his reach. Then again, I must liberate the toy for him, or he will whine in frustration.

Darwin has a crate that he likes to sleep in. It's fairly small, and I can easily move it from room to room. Darwin goes down for the night around eight o'clock, so if I want to watch TV or listen to music later than that, I move the crate to a room where he will not be bothered by the noise. When his bedtime comes, I get out a teeth-cleaning treat that he can gnaw on while he settles down to sleep. Darwin loves this little ritual and rushes to his crate to be there in time to receive the treat. Even if he has just seen me move the crate to another room, however, he will invariably look for it in its usual place before eventually finding his way to the new spot.

I have met several other beagle owners, and they all tell me that, while their pets are very sweet and affectionate, they have the brainpower of a rock. So, I have to assume that dog thinking is more complicated than I imagined. I see that I have a lot of work ahead of me before I can fit my findings on Darwin's communication skills into a broader framework of canine intelligence.

I was really touched that Darwin told me he considers me a friend. I always suspected that he had feelings for me, but it was nice to hear him say it. Dogs can send such mixed messages. Darwin loves to jump up on my lap for a cuddle, and he always wags his tail excitedly when I come home from work.

His apparent affection for me, however, does not preclude him from constantly doing things he knows I don't like. When he runs around the living room, he always manages to displace the sofa and coffee table and scrunch up the area rug so that I have to put them all back in order if I want to sit down to listen to some music. It's always a struggle to get him into his harness when we go for walks. He turns his head away from the opening at the front of the harness and tries to start running to the door before I have snapped the fasteners on either side. If I forget to close my bedroom door, he invariably sneaks in and grabs a dirty sock out of the laundry basket and rips it to shreds. All this despite the fact that I chastise him every time he pulls one of these stunts.

My friends with children tell me similar stories about how their kids can be all hugs and kisses one minute and creating havoc the next. I guess that's why so many couples get a dog before they start having children—it's good practice!

December 18, 2023

I had a chance to talk to Diane today and thank her again for lending Fluffy to me to help with the podcast. I told her, though, that while Fluffy cooperated quite well, we were not able to complete the recording with her. Diane was disappointed but was glad to hear that Darwin had ended his strike. She had listened to the earlier episodes of the podcast, thought they were wonderful, and was looking forward to hearing more. I think she was sorry that Fluffy would not be featured in future episodes, but she wished me good luck with my experiments.

Diane and I got talking about Christmas, and she mentioned that, since her kids had spent Thanksgiving with her, they would be at their father's house for Christmas Day. I suggested she come over to my place for lunch, and she agreed. She admitted she wasn't a great cook but that she would be happy to bring some wine and a cake from the bakery. I knew her taste in wine was excellent, so I readily agreed. I'm not that adept in the kitchen myself, but with a week to prepare, I should be able to come up with something tasty.

I also encouraged her to bring Fluffy along. I didn't tell her that Fluffy had expressed fear of Darwin. I am hoping that, if those two get to know each other better, they will become friends. It would be nice for Darwin to have someone to hang out with sometimes while I'm at work.

Chapter 17

Darwin on Life
Episode 9: Merry Christmas, Darwin!

[Opening theme music]

VO: *Darwin on Life*: Man and dog at the dawn of a new age.

Walker Grant: Welcome back to *Darwin on Life*! I am your host, Walker Grant, and I am here with my partner, Darwin, to advance our explorations into interspecies communication. As regular listeners know, Darwin is a beagle. We are able to speak to each other thanks to the app I have created that uses artificial intelligence to convert canine vocalizations into human speech.

So, Darwin, Christmas is just around the corner. Are you excited?

Darwin: I am absolutely giddy with anticipation.

WG: That's funny, you don't sound especially giddy. Your tone of voice sounds more blasé to me. Do you like Christmas, or are you more of a Scrooge or a Grinch?

Darwin: I am definitely not a Scrooge. Isn't he a duck?

WG: I think you are getting your Scrooges mixed up. Scrooge Mc-Duck is a Disney cartoon character. He is the uncle of Donald Duck. He takes his name from the original Scrooge, Ebenezer Scrooge, a miserly old man in the Charles Dickens story "A Christmas Carol."

Darwin: Ah, yes, the very near-sighted fellow who goes around saying, "Bah, humbug!"

WG: You're on the right track, but you must be thinking of the cartoon version of the story where Mr. Magoo plays the part of Ebenezer Scrooge.

Darwin: Hold on. Mr. Magoo, a cartoon, plays the part of a fictional character—in a cartoon? That doesn't make any sense. Why didn't they just make a cartoon Ebenezer Scrooge?

WG: Hmm. Good question, I never thought about that. I guess they thought that if they used a popular cartoon character, then more people would watch the show.

Darwin: They should have used Snoopy instead. Everyone loves Snoopy!

WG: That's true, but it would have seemed a little weird to have a nice dog like Snoopy running a money-lending business where he treated his employees harshly.

Darwin: Weirder than having Snoopy be a World War I flying ace who shoots down enemy aircraft? But you're right, Snoopy is too lovable to be a convincing Scrooge.

WG: So then, are you a Grinch? Does all the noisy celebration of Christmas annoy you?

Darwin: Not really. Not that the Grinch is all bad, mind you. His only friend is a dog, after all. Although he doesn't treat him very well. Like all dogs, Max is very loyal to his companion, but the Grinch still tries to exploit him by making him pull a sleigh filled with toys. That's a job for eight reindeer. Nine if you include Rudolph. I can empathize with Max. I know what it feels like to have someone take advantage of my loyalty.

WG: Mm-hmm. Let's move on. So why aren't you more excited about Christmas?

Darwin: Well, I've only experienced one Christmas so far, and that was kind of a mixed bag. As you will recall, you went to see your family last year, so I stayed with my sitters, Penny and Patty. It was fun being there with all the other dogs, and the ladies made special Christmas dog treats that were super yummy. The dog biscuits with liver-pâté icing were my favorites.

WG: They really do spoil you over there. But what didn't you like?

Darwin: They made us all dress up in ugly Christmas sweaters. They took pictures of all of us that they posted to Facebook and Instagram. I didn't think much of it at the time since I was such a young puppy. But my dog friends still tease me about it. It has been very humiliating, and I really don't want to go through that again.

WG: That is certainly understandable. Well then, you will be happy to know that this year I am staying home, and I promise you I won't dress you up in any way that displeases you. Our neighbor Diane will come over for Christmas lunch, and I told her that her dog Fluffy was welcome to join us. I'm sure you remember Fluffy, right?

Darwin: How could I forget? Fluffy, the scab who tried to usurp my place in the podcast.

WG: You really can't blame Fluffy. It was all my idea to involve her in the podcast after you went on strike. Please be nice to her. She is a bit afraid of you, and I would really prefer that she not do an anxiety pee on my carpet. It is almost impossible to get out the smell afterward.

Darwin: OK. I will be a perfect gentlehound. Besides, even though Fluffy is by no means my intellectual equal, she is kind of cute. I wouldn't mind snuggling up with her by the fireplace. I'm thinking an Arthur Miller/Marilyn Monroe kind of relationship.

WG: You be careful, Darwin! I don't want you to go breaking any hearts, especially on Christmas Day. Oh no, now I've got that Wham! song stuck in my head. [Walker sings.] Last Christmas, I gave you my heart, baddah baddah de dah, baddah baddah de dee. I never can remember the words.

Darwin: Gross. Now you've infected me, too. Can you put on some other Christmas music that will push that annoying tune out of my head?

WG: Sorry, Darwin, I can't put on any music while we are recording this podcast because I can't afford the royalties.

Darwin: We definitely need to get some corporate sponsors and pronto. How about if we sing some traditional Christmas carols? They are all in the public domain, so it won't cost us anything.

WG: I'm not sure our audience is really interested in hearing us sing Christmas carols, but I am curious to know which ones you like.

Darwin: Not surprisingly, I have a soft spot for Christmas songs that recognize the important role that animals have played in making Christmas such a special time. The best of all is "Soul Cake." The first verse goes like this:

[Darwin sings]

God bless the master of this house
And the mistress also
And all the little children
That round your table grow
The cattle in your stable
The dog at your front door
And all that dwell within your gates
We'll wish you ten times more.

Can you imagine how wonderful it would be to live in a house with ten dogs? I get a little misty-eyed just thinking about it.

WG: And I get a little terrified. All the barking and howling and furniture chewing. No offense, Darwin, but looking after one dog is challenging enough. Ten would drive me around the bend.

Darwin: Not that anyone would notice. But, hey, it was just a thought.

WG: Any other Christmas songs on your top ten list?

Darwin: "The Friendly Beasts" is another great one. It doesn't mention dogs specifically, but pay attention to the last verse:

[Darwin sings]

Every beast by some good spell
In the stable dark was glad to tell
Of the gifts they gave Emanuel.
The gifts they gave Emanuel.

So, I am sure there must have been a dog in the manger. Let me rephrase that. I am sure there must have been a dog looking after the baby Jesus. He probably made sure that no cat jumped on the Christ child's face. It wouldn't do to have the Messiah smothered to death on the day he was born.

WG: Darwin, that fear about cats smothering babies is just an urban legend. You'd better be more careful what you say about cats if you expect them to support your presidential ambitions.

Darwin: Good point. "Sorry" to all you cats listening out there. I will make it up to you when I am in the White House. My first presidential act will be to mandate that all cats get cream instead of milk in their bowls. I'm sure no other presidential candidate will be willing to make that promise!

WG: You are surely correct on that score, Darwin. Say, we have only a few minutes left. Is there any gift you would especially like for Christmas? Nothing too expensive, I hope.

Darwin: Oh, Walker, you know me. I have very simple tastes. A new blanket would be nice. I'm afraid I may have gotten a little too aggressive with my old one. It's more holes than blanket at this point.

WG: New blanket, check. That shouldn't be a problem. Anything else?

Darwin: I could definitely use a new collar. The one I have is so 2022. I saw one on TV the other day that was genuine leather with in-set rhinestones. The jewels would really bring out the sparkle in my eyes.

WG: Vanity, thy name is Darwin. OK. Let me see what I can find.

Darwin: And, of course, I would still like a brand-new Tesla Model S Plaid with a personal chauffeur. The highway's siren call is taunting me. I long to feel the wind rushing through my fur as I stick my head out the passenger side window to soak in all the wondrous odors of the road.

WG: Keep dreaming. Tell you what. When we go for our afternoon walk, I will let you linger over the smells coming from our street. I think I saw a dead raccoon there this morning. That should set your olfactory system all aflutter.

Darwin: I should probably be upset with you for that bit of sarcasm, but *eau de raton laveur mort* sounds captivating.

WG: OK, Darwin, it's time to say goodbye to our listeners. Darwin and I wish you all the happiest of holidays and good health and good fortune in the new year.

Darwin: [Singing] Soul a soul a soul cake. Please, good missus, a soul cake. An apple, a pear, a plum or a cherry, any good thing to make us all merry...

[Outro music; credits]

Chapter 18

December 26, 2023

I have to say that was one of the nicest Christmases I have ever spent! Right after breakfast, Darwin and I went into the living room where I had set up the tree. It's a plastic one that I put out every year because I can't be bothered to purchase and decorate a real one. It's a small tree, just big enough to shelter the small pile of presents that I receive from my family every year. I gave Darwin the blanket and collar he requested. I put a little dog treat in each package to entice him to open them. I think he enjoys ripping off the wrapping paper as much as getting the presents.

My parents sent me a small set of basic tools. My father visited me a few months ago and saw that one of the kitchen cabinet doors had fallen off its hinges. He was appalled when I told him that I hadn't gotten around to fixing it yet because I didn't have a screwdriver. So, it was a slightly barbed gift, but I must admit the tools will come in handy.

My brother and his wife sent me a rather expensive fitness watch. It can tell me how many steps I have taken and how many calories I have burned, and it monitors my heart rate. I am sure it does dozens of other things, but I doubt I will ever read the instruction manual to find out. For that matter, I don't imagine I will ever wear the watch, as

I am not really a fitness buff. My brother, of course, knows this, so his gift is more a commentary on my lifestyle than an expression of love.

The one truly great gift was the sweater that my sister Gina knitted for me. It is just my size and has the V-neck that I prefer. She used a very soft, merino wool yarn, and the color is a forest green that looks good on me. I am sure I will wear it often this winter.

Diane and Fluffy came over shortly before noon. Diane brought two bottles of wine—a white and a red, since, as she said, she wasn't sure what I was going to make. The white was an elegant French sauvignon blanc that paired perfectly with the shrimp dish I made for lunch. The red was an aromatic Bordeaux that we enjoyed with the Death by Chocolate cake she brought for dessert. Both wines served to relax us enough that conversation flowed freely and was punctuated by a lot of laughter.

Much to my relief, Darwin and Fluffy got over their mutual mistrust. They spent most of the day chasing each other around the yard and playing tug-of-war with one of Darwin's chew toys. After lunch, while Diane and I polished off the rest of the wine, Darwin and Fluffy curled up in front of the fireplace next to each other and had a nap. The crackling sounds of the fire served as a soothing soundtrack for the afternoon.

Diane and I shared some of our personal histories with each other. She grew up in a small town that she had rarely left before going off to college. She was always a bookworm and, like me, had trouble making friends with the other kids at school. They weren't especially mean to her; they just were not as interesting as the characters in the novels she loved.

Diane met her ex-husband, Lou, the first week of college, and they started dating right away. Lou was her first boyfriend, and she said she spent a lot of time trying to figure out how she should act with him. Fortunately, the girls at the college had much more in common with her than did her high school cohort, so she had lots of friends who were more than happy to guide her through the maze of young love. She used air quotes when she said "love." She liked Lou because he was very gentle and patient with her and because they had similar tastes in literature. But she admitted she always had doubts as to whether they were really in love with each other.

Looking back, Diane said, what she was really in love with was the whole college scene. Lou had lots of friends from his dorm, and that group and Diane's friends made a point of always eating dinner together at the same dining hall every night. They were a boisterous group, and Diane loved the constant joking and ribbing that bound the group together. She said she realized years later that she had projected this warm feeling onto Lou and had conflated her joy at being part of this family of friends with affection for him.

Diane and Lou remained a couple throughout college, and, when graduation was approaching, she was not surprised that Lou proposed. She had already chatted at length with her girlfriends as to how she should respond, and they all assured her that Lou was a great catch and that she should take the chance.

The wedding was held a few months after graduation. Diane got pregnant during their honeymoon in the Bahamas. Lou worked as an accountant, and they bought a comfortable home in the suburbs. Diane was a stay-at-home mom while the kids were little, but eventually found work in television advertising. Having children served much the same function as having a group of mutual friends had done during college—it gave Lou and Diane a shared interest and helped them keep at bay any thought that they were not right for each other.

Eventually, the invisible cords that had always been pulling Diane and Lou in opposite directions caused a tear in their relationship. The rupture came about for a reason that Diane could never have imagined. One day, a couple of years ago, Lou came home from work to declare that he was now to be called Louise and that he would be living as a woman. He said he understood that this would come as a shock to Diane, but he hoped they could continue to live together as a loving couple.

Diane said that her first reaction to this news was to have some kind of out-of-body experience. She said she felt as though she were watching a couple of characters in an avant-garde movie talking to each other through a long tube that distorted their voices so they could not understand each other. When she regained her equilibrium, she told her husband that she needed some time to think through what he had just told her. In fact, she told me she knew right away that his proposal would never work, and that the only sensible thing for them to do was to split up.

As I sat there, slack-jawed, trying to get my head around this revelation, Diane asked me, "So, have you ever been married?"

"Yes," I told her. "But I'm afraid my story will seem pretty pedestrian compared to yours."

She smiled and said, "Don't worry, it's not a competition."

So, I told her that, about twenty years earlier, I met a woman named Lorna through a matchmaking service for academics. We dated for a while and got along well enough that we decided to marry. Lorna was very keen on having a child—in retrospect, I think it was her desire to be a mother that pushed her to the altar more than any passion for me. Unfortunately, our efforts to procreate were in vain. We both went to our doctors for help, and it turned out I have a very low sperm count.

We looked into treatment options, but before we got very far down that road, things took an unexpected turn. Lorna traveled to an academic conference out of state. Several weeks later, she told me she was leaving and wanted a divorce. She gave me only the vaguest reason why, and packed her things and drove away. I later found out that she had a fling during the conference, and her paramour apparently had all the sperm necessary. The relationship with the lover didn't last, but Lorna got the baby she wanted. The whole experience soured my view of love and marriage, and I have devoted myself to my research ever since.

Diane was quiet for a moment, then looked up with a wry smile on her face. "It's funny," she said. "We try to prepare ourselves for life's inevitable hardships. We buy health insurance knowing we might get sick, and life insurance knowing that our spouses might die. We put aside a little money each month in case we lose our jobs or our cars break down. But life has a way of throwing things at us that we didn't even know were possible. So, we are completely unprepared when they hit us, and at a loss to know how to carry on when they do. But we do carry on. I'm not sure why or how, but we do."

December 31, 2023

I have invited some of my colleagues from the university over to my house to celebrate New Year's Eve tonight. They are all single guys like me, and we have a tradition of ringing in the new year together since, frankly, we don't have any place else to go. I agreed to host this year because I want them to see my recording setup and perhaps give me some ideas as to what direction I should take with the podcast. I have a sense that I need to be a little more rigorous in guiding the conversations, but it is hard for me to stay on track once Darwin gets wound up on a particular topic. My colleagues have taken little interest in my work to date, but I hope that a glimpse of how the sausage is made will move them into my camp.

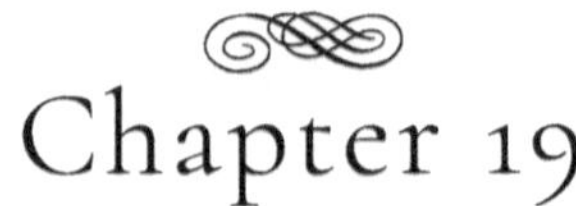

Chapter 19

Darwin on Life
Episode 10: Darwin's New Year's Resolutions

[Opening theme music]

VO: *Darwin on Life*: Man and dog at the dawn of a new age.

Darwin: Happy New Year, everybody! Darwin here. Regular listeners will be surprised to hear me leading off the podcast. I will explain the situation in just a moment.

For any of you new to *Darwin on Life*, let me give you a little background. I am a beagle. I don't talk in the traditional sense. This is not by any means a *Mr. Ed* reboot. My partner, Walker, who normally hosts this podcast, invented an app that uses artificial intelligence to convert my vocalizations into recognizable human speech. Walker is an odd duck, but I must admit his app works remarkably well. Thanks to his invention, I have had the opportunity to share my thoughts on a wide range of subjects. Please check out the earlier podcast episodes to hear me wax eloquent on a variety of topics, including labor relations, global warming, and presidential politics. I have no doubt you will find my insights fascinating.

Anyway, I suppose you are wondering where Walker is. I am sorry to report that he is a bit under the weather today. He invited some of his professor friends over to celebrate New Year's Eve last night, and things got a little out of hand. Who would have thought that a bunch of nerdy science guys could raise such a ruckus? Several of them are still conked out in random corners of the house, most of them with dollops of guacamole dip festooning their vestments.

Oh, wait, I think I hear Walker stumbling this way. Let's see if he is up to taking over the hosting duties. Oh, Walker, do you realize it is almost noon? Time to get rolling!

Walker Grant: Oh, my aching head. I feel like I have a gerbil in my mouth. Good morning, Darwin. How was your—say, wait a minute. I understood what you said. Are you talking into the app?

Darwin: No, silly, I wished on a star that I could speak like a real boy, and Jiminy Cricket granted my request. Of course I'm speaking through the app.

WG: But how did you manage to turn it on?

Darwin: I didn't. You and your professor buddies were playing around with it last night, and you forgot to turn it off when you went to sleep. You all took turns trying to talk like a dog to see what the app would produce. I recommend you delete the recordings as soon as possible. If anyone on the college board of trustees were to hear them, your careers would be toast.

WG: Toast. Yes, I think I could handle a slice of toast. Actually, what I really need is a little hair of the dog that bit me.

Darwin: You stay away from my fur, you cannibal! The only reason I bit you was because you put antlers on my head, and you and your friends started shooting at me with Nerf guns while singing "Run, Run, Rudolph" at the top of your lungs. To coin a phrase, "We were not amused!"

WG: Oh, that explains the puncture wound on my thumb. But I just meant I may need a little of what I drank last night to get rid of this hangover. At least that's what people say. It's probably just an old wives' tale, but I'm open to anything at the moment. I think I saw a bit of Frozen Mudslide left in the blender. Let me get some of that. I'll be right back.

Darwin: Don't take too long, I'm not sure our audience will be willing to wait for you. It is New Year's Day after all. There are parades and football to be watched.

WG: Our audience? Darwin, have you been recording all along?

Darwin: Well, someone had to do it, and none of your professor friends is awake yet.

WG: Oh my God! I need to get into my chair. This is so embarrassing. [Sound of Walker clearing his throat.] Happy New Year, everybody! And welcome to *Darwin on*—

Darwin: We've already done that bit. We're at the part where you ask me some uninspired question and I extemporize a thought-provoking disquisition on a more scintillating topic.

WG: Darwin, would you mind speaking in slightly less florid language today? I'm not sure my head can handle your eloquence.

Darwin: Fine. What would you like to talk about?

WG: Let me think. You've caught me a bit off guard. I know. Since it's New Year's, why don't you tell me if you've made any resolutions? Is that something dogs do?

Darwin: It's not part of our heritage. Dogs are pretty much perfect the way they are. We don't really need self-improvement. But, as a matter of fact, we do take the opportunity of a new year dawning to set goals for ourselves. Even dogs need to have some focus.

WG: That sounds like a good approach. What are some of your goals?

Darwin: As you know, I have a number of creative projects in the works. We have discussed my memoir. I'm afraid I have not made as much progress as I would like, so I am thinking of changing it up a little. I propose to keep an audio journal of my daily reflections. I will set aside a few minutes every day to memorialize my thoughts on whatever strikes my fancy. I figure by the end of the year, I should have enough material for volume one. I will hire a ghost writer to put it all in order for me. I don't really enjoy the organizing aspect. I'm more of a big picture kind of dog. Is it all right if I use your recording equipment for this project?

WG: Thanks for asking, although I have a feeling you would have used it anyway. Sure, go right ahead.

Darwin: Much obliged. While we are on the topic of recording, I have some ideas for the next Darwin and the Finches album. I want to move in a more classical music direction. Rex, Daisy, and I are stronger on vocals than instrumental music, so I am working on a choral work that should be better suited to our talents. I call it *A Feather on the Breath of Dog.*

WG: Aren't you afraid some people might consider that title sacrilegious?

Darwin: What do you mean?

WG: Never mind. Sure, you can record that, too. Just do me a favor and try to keep Rex from slobbering on the microphone.

Darwin: I'll do my best. He is a golden retriever, though. Drool is in his blood. Not literally, of course, but you know what I mean.

WG: Any other goals for the new year?

Darwin: I'm starting to feel a little sluggish after all the good food I ate over the holidays, so I think I need to get more exercise.

WG: That sounds like a good idea. I could use more exercise, too. I can use the watch my brother gave me for Christmas to keep track of my progress. Shall we extend our walks by another ten minutes or so?

Darwin: I was thinking of something more in the sports line.

WG: Oh, like fetch? Do you want me to throw a ball for you?

Darwin: Fetch is for puppies. That would bore me to tears.

WG: OK. How about Frisbee? I see a lot of dogs playing Frisbee in the park. It looks like they are having fun.

Darwin: Walker, have you looked at me lately? I am a beagle. I am rather close to the ground. Jumping is not really my thing.

WG: All right, then, what sport would you like to take up?

Darwin: I'll give you a clue. Its name has a connection to a dog.

WG: I hope you don't mean sled dog racing. You know how I hate the cold. Besides, you need a whole team of dogs to do sled dog racing.

Darwin: No, no, I don't mean sled dog racing, although that does sound like a lot of fun. I'm talking about pickleball.

WG: Pickleball? What does that have to do with dogs?

Darwin: Well, there is a bit of controversy there. One of the families that invented the game claims the name came from a pickle boat race, although it's not entirely clear to me what one has to do with the other. The other family used to say that they named the game after their dog Pickles because he liked to pick up the ball and run away with it. They later admitted, though, that they didn't get Pickles until a couple of years after they invented the game. So, Pickles was more likely named after the game than the other way around.

WG: No offense, Darwin, but how can you play pickleball? You don't have hands.

Darwin: Who says you need hands? I can just hold the racket in my mouth.

WG: I know I have some pickleball equipment around here somewhere. Let me see. Oh, here it is. Here, take this racket and show me what you can do. I'll toss you the ball and—wow, you really smashed it!

Darwin: Are you surprised? Serving might be a challenge, but I think that if I use my front paw to push the ball up on the racket, then drop the ball on the ground, I can serve it off the bounce. What say we head over to the neighborhood pickleball court and play a few games?

WG: Maybe after I've had my coffee. Say, let me look at that racket. Jeez, Darwin, you've completely chewed it up.

Darwin: It's not chewed up. I simply modified the handle to fit my mouth shape. It's like the way you put special grips on your golf clubs to accommodate your tiny little hands.

WG: I do not have tiny little hands! Thank goodness I have another pickleball racket. Please do not modify that one, OK?

Darwin: Word.

WG: Well, Darwin, I see by the timer on the recording app that we are at the end of another episode. Shall we wish our audience a "Happy New Year?"

Darwin: How about we sing a little "Auld Lang Syne?" I need to warm up my voice before I practice my choral work.

WG: No, thanks. I'm afraid when we get to the "cup of kindness" part, I may toss my cookies. Happy New Year, everybody!

Darwin: [Singing] Should old acquaintance be forgot and never brought to mind...

[Outro music; credits]

Chapter 20

January 4, 2024

Well, New Year's was certainly a bust. I hoped my professor friends would finally take an interest in my work once they saw the rigor of my experiments. But no, they acted like silly schoolboys with a new toy. Darwin was right, they sounded like complete idiots barking into the microphone. I had to apologize to Darwin for dressing him up like a reindeer and shooting Nerf darts at him. I know how much he hates cosplay, but I'm afraid that after a few drinks, my decision-making was not at its best.

To make things up to him, I took Darwin to the pickleball court so we could test his skills. It was a little awkward at first, but he managed to get the hang of it quite quickly. We tried to play an actual game, but it soon became clear we would have to modify the rules to accommodate his limitations. We agreed that Darwin doesn't have to get his serves into the correct section of the court—anything that goes over the net is fair play. I also pledged that I would always try to hit the ball so that it lands in front of him, as he can't really manage a shot while running away from the net. With those few changes in place, we had a fun afternoon.

As we were leaving the pickleball court, we ran into Diane, who was going to play with some lady friends. She had brought Fluffy along to watch, so I suggested she let her play, too, using the modified rules to which Darwin and I had agreed. She gave me a quizzical look but said she would give it a try. The next day, she called, and it was clear she was in a good mood. She said that she tried to get Fluffy to play, and, much to her surprise, she took to pickleball like a fish to water. She and Fluffy hadn't had so much fun together in a long time, and she thanked me profusely for my suggestion. The reason she called, she said, was not only to thank me but to invite Darwin and me to a match. I readily agreed, so we will get together later this week. I'm sure Darwin will be delighted.

Chapter 21

Darwin on Life
Episode 11: Darwin Scores a Touchdown

[Opening theme music]

VO: *Darwin on Life*: Man and dog at the dawn of a new age.

Walker Grant: Hello there. Walker Grant here, the host of *Darwin on Life*. Darwin will be joining us shortly. He's still licking his wounds from our pickleball game with our neighbor Diane and her dog Fluffy. When I say "licking his wounds," I mean that both literally and figuratively. He lunged for a ball and landed awkwardly, scraping his left front paw. He's also upset because Fluffy is a much better pickleball player than he is. Their team beat us in five straight games. I think Darwin may have exaggerated the extent of his injury just so we would stop playing.

Oh, here he comes now. Say, Darwin, that was quite the match, wouldn't you say?

Darwin: I don't want to talk about it.

WG: How's your paw? Is it still bleeding?

Darwin: No, I licked it clean. There's nothing better for a wound than a little dog spittle.

WG: That's good. Still, I'll take a look at it after the podcast. I have some antiseptic cream that might help prevent an infection.

Darwin: I doubt Big Pharma has come up with anything more effective than dog drool. I just need to stay off that paw for a few weeks, so don't be surprised to see me limping around for a while.

WG: Gosh, that's a shame. Diane and Fluffy invited us for a rematch this weekend. I was hoping we could practice a bit and maybe give them a more competitive game. But if you're not up for it, I understand.

Darwin: Oh, I'm up for it all right. It's just that it's important to be sure the injury is completely healed before returning to competition. Just look at Tiger Woods. He would probably have three more majors under his belt if he hadn't tried to play golf again so soon after his back surgery.

WG: Well, I'm glad you will be looking after yourself. I thought maybe you were afraid that Fluffy would show you up again. She has an amazing backhand shot. Or should I call it a backmouth shot since she holds the paddle with her teeth?

Darwin: Yes, she did take a few lucky swipes at the ball. I purposely wasn't playing my A game until I had a chance to assess her skills. Pickleball is supposed to be a fun, social game, so I didn't want to discourage her by blowing all my shots past her.

WG: That's funny. It looked to me like you blew quite a few of your shots.

Darwin: [Expletives deleted.]

WG: Hey, calm down. I was just teasing. Tell you what. There are a lot of pickleball instructional videos on YouTube. Let's watch a few to get some pointers. Once your paw heals, we can head back to the court and do some practice sessions on our own. I'm sure with a little practice, we will be able to hold our own against Diane and Fluffy. What do you say?

Darwin: That sounds like a good idea. I thought the game would be mostly strategy, which would have given us an advantage given our superior intellects. But I see now that it is important to master the basic shots.

WG: Do I detect a bit of a sexist attitude there? "Our superior intellects?"

Darwin: Actually, I was including you just to be polite. I think we have established that beagles really stand out in the cognition department.

WG: Whatever. Anyway, pickleball will be more fun once the weather warms up. Right now, I want to set aside time to watch the NFL playoffs and the Super Bowl. That will keep me occupied for the next few weekends. How about you? Are you a football fan?

Darwin: Sure, I like football, especially when I can watch it at my sitters, Penny and Patty's house. They serve these football-shaped dog treats made with peanut butter that are scrumpsheroo. They also have some rubber footballs that they throw around the yard for the dogs to catch. As you know, I'm not much for playing fetch, but we turn it into a contest by seeing who can get to the football first. I don't mean to brag, but the other dogs refer to me as Stefon Dog for my skills as a wide receiver.

WG: Stefon Dog? Oh, I get it, like Stefon Diggs for the Buffalo Bills. Are the Bills your favorite NFL team?

Darwin: I don't really have a favorite. I am upset that no NFL team has had the good sense to name itself after a dog. I mean, you have a whole flock of birds—Eagles, Falcons, Seahawks, Cardinals, and Ravens. And way too many cats—Jaguars, Lions, Panthers, and Bengals. I was excited when the Washington team changed its name to the Commanders, because I thought it was named for Joe Biden's dog. Then I found out the name was meant to highlight Washington's connection to the military. That was quite a letdown.

WG: Now that you mention it, considering how popular dogs are, it is a little strange that no team has chosen a dog name. I suppose you would like to see a team call itself the Beagles, right? Like the Boise Beagles or the Brooklyn Beagles? Alliterative team names are quite popular.

Darwin: Those names do have a lovely ring to them. But beagles are known more for their intelligence and sophistication than their aggressiveness. I would certainly understand if a team preferred to choose the name of a breed that highlighted its toughness. Since Pittsburgh isn't much of a steel town anymore, its team could change its name from the Steelers to the Pit Bulls. The Pittsburgh Pit Bulls, that rolls off the tongue nicely and should strike fear into the hearts of their opponents.

Or maybe now that Donald Trump has shanghaied the word "patriot" to mean someone who attacked the Capitol, New England might want to change its team name to the Rottweilers. They could have helmets with a snarling Rottweiler on them. Do you think any opposing team would relish facing down that front line?

WG: We should contact the new United Football League to give them some suggestions. None of the first eight teams has a dog name, but I suspect the league will grow if it has any success.

Darwin: I have an even better idea. How about if we start the Canine Football League or CFL? It would be the first all-animal sports league. I have no doubt it would be extremely popular. We could get a lot of big corporate sponsors like Purina and Chewy. I'm sure the networks would bid up the rights to broadcast our games. It would be like the Puppy Bowl on steroids. We could make a fortune!

WG: Not to rain on your parade, but I foresee a few problems with your grand scheme.

Darwin: I'm sure you do, Debbie Downer. What problems do you foresee?

WG: Well, to start with, you probably don't want to call it the CFL because people will confuse that with the Canadian Football League.

Darwin: Oh, right. All seventeen of their fans might become nonplussed. Fine, we'll call it the DFL for Dog Football League. That's better anyway. We don't want any wolves or dingoes to think they might be eligible to play.

WG: What do you have against wolves and dingoes?

Darwin: Nothing. They are perfectly fine species. It's just that they are, shall we say, undomesticated. I don't think we can trust them to follow the rules, especially the rule against eating members of the opposing team. I mean, would you want gorillas and orangutans playing in the NFL?

WG: I guess you're right. But how can dogs even play football? There's no way a dog quarterback could throw a forward pass. And I can't imagine a dog place kicker sending a field goal through the uprights.

Darwin: Obviously, we would have to modify the rules. You know, back in the old days, there was no forward pass in football. We would be returning football to its roots. We could also lower the bar of the goal posts so that a dog could kick the ball over. If you haven't figured it out by now, we dogs are very capable of adapting human inventions to meet our unique skill sets.

WG: You mean like how you adapt furniture legs to be chew toys? Or how you adapt tennis shoes to be chew toys? Or how you adapt practically everything in the house to be a chew toy?

Darwin: Do I detect a hint of bitterness in that comment? Chewing is a natural behavior for dogs. Puppies chew to relieve the pain of teething. All dogs chew when they are bored or stressed. If you humans want to keep us dogs as companions, you just need to ensure that we have a steady supply of acceptable chew toys.

WG: Thanks for the advice. OK, one more concern. You say you want to name the teams after dog breeds, but will you require each team to consist entirely of dogs of that breed? Wouldn't that give some teams an unfair advantage? I mean, wouldn't the Green Bay Great Danes be a safe bet against the Denver Dachshunds?

Darwin: Don't be so sure. Dachshunds make for cagey running backs. They can scoot right between the legs of taller breeds. But don't forget, dog-breed names are purely human inventions. We dogs see each other as equals, all members of the canine brotherhood. We would use the breed names solely as marketing tools to get more humans to watch the games. We would, of course, draft players based on their individual talents without regard to breed. Heck, most of the players wouldn't even be identifiable as a specific breed. Some of the best football players I know are mutts. And the word "mutt" is not a pejorative among us dogs.

WG: Well, Darwin, as always, you have given me a lot to think about. Maybe I can talk to some of the other folks at the dog park about setting up a dog football league there as a proof of concept. You can work with your dog friends to come up with some adaptations to the rules.

Right now, however, I am going to grab a beer and get ready for the next NFL playoff game. Thanks to our audience for tuning in. Have a great week, and please keep an eye out for the next episode of *Darwin on Life*. Goodbye!

Darwin: [Singing] On, Wisconsin! On, Wisconsin! Plunge right through that line! Run the ball clear down the field, a touchdown sure this time...

[Outro music; credits]

✦

Chapter 22

January 7, 2024

I got a call from Diane this morning. I could tell from her voice that she was excited by what she had to say. She had spoken to the host of the morning show on her TV station about Darwin and me and our experiments in interspecies communication. The show is called *Coffee and Tina* and is hosted by local media personality Tina Gray. Ms. Gray often invites local people on to talk about their hobbies and interests in a segment she calls "Community Canvas." Diane gave Tina the link to our podcast, and, after listening to a few episodes, Tina agreed that Darwin and I might make interesting guests.

Diane told me that Tina would be calling me in the next couple of days to discuss a possible appearance on her show and, perhaps, even to set up a time for the taping. The "Community Canvas" segments are taped, Diane said, because most of the guests are not experienced with live TV. They used to do the segments live, but too many guests either froze up in front of the cameras or blathered on about their interests without giving Tina a chance to ask questions. By taping, the producers can do several takes if necessary to give the guests their best chance of making a good impression. They tape a week's worth of segments back-to-back to take advantage of the presence of a small studio audience.

I was stunned by this news, but remembered in the nick of time to thank Diane for setting up this opportunity. She said she thought Darwin and I would be a big hit and wished us well. I decided to wait until I spoke with Tina before mentioning any of this to Darwin. I knew he would be over the moon with a chance to be on TV, so I didn't want to get his hopes up in case it fell through.

January 8, 2024

Tina Gray called me this morning to get some background on my experiments with Darwin. I got the impression she was also scoping me out to be sure I wasn't some kind of weirdo. She had listened to a few of the podcast episodes and told me she had found them to be delightful. She said she hoped Darwin would be equally forthcoming on her show. I explained to Tina in a very general way how I used AI to convert Darwin's utterances to human speech. I also assured her that Darwin would be an eager participant.

I must have made a good impression on Tina as she asked me right then if Darwin and I would be available on Wednesday afternoon to do the taping. She told me to wear solid colors (no green) and mentioned that they would do a little makeup on me before the taping. She asked if Darwin or I needed anything in particular. I said I would bring my laptop that has the AI program loaded onto it and that she could connect that to the studio's audio input. I asked her if there was a grassy spot outside the studio where Darwin could relieve himself, and she assured me there was. I told her I would bring some little dog treats that she could give to Darwin to help win him over. I thanked her for inviting us on the show and said I looked forward to meeting her on Wednesday.

I called Diane to tell her the good news. She was thrilled and said she would meet Darwin and me at the station to guide us to the right studio. I also told Darwin, who ran around in circles for nearly a minute, letting out little yelps of joy as he spun. I really hope this goes well. This could be a big break to help me get some long-over-due recognition. It will also be an opportunity to give Darwin his star turn.

Chapter 23

Coffee and Tina
"Community Canvas" segment for January 15, 2024

Unedited transcript

Tina Gray: Good morning, again, and welcome to "Community Canvas." My guests today are Professor Walker Grant and his dog, Darwin. Professor—

Walker Grant: Sorry, but would you mind not referring to Darwin as "my dog." He is very sensitive about his personal agency.

TG: Uh, OK. How should I introduce him?

WG: You can just say, "Professor Walker Grant and Darwin." I'm sure your audience will pick up on the fact that he is a dog.

TG: Of course. Let's start again.

Good morning, again, and welcome to "Community Canvas." My guests today are Professor Walker Grant and Darwin. Please give them a warm welcome. [Applause]

Professor Grant, please tell us a little—

WG: Please, call me Walker.

TG: OK, but we only have a short time to do this taping. So if you could please refrain from any unnecessary interruptions—

WG: I'm sorry, of course. Please go ahead.

TG: Thank you.

Walker, please tell us about your work on interspecies communication. Do I understand correctly that you have developed an app for this purpose?

WG: That's right, Tina. May I call you Tina?

TG: Of course, Walker. Please go on.

WG: Well, Tina, as you say, I created an app that used artificial intelligence to analyze thousands of hours of canine communication that I have collected over the course of my career. As a result, when Darwin speaks into the microphone connected to my computer, the app translates what he says into recognizable human speech.

TG: Fascinating. Well, with that background in mind, let's see what Darwin has to say to us today. Darwin, good morning, and thanks for joining us today on "Community Canvas." Is there something you would like to say to our audience?

Darwin: Good morning, Tina. It is a real pleasure for me to be here. I have been a fan of *Coffee and Tina* for a long time now. It's the first thing I watch when Walker and I get back from our morning walk. I have learned a lot about our community from your show. The segment you did last week on the dangers of chemical fertilizers couldn't have been more informative. Fortunately, my sensitive nose can detect when a lawn has been recently fertilized, so I can avoid walking on it. Since I don't wear shoes, those chemicals could do a real number on my tender paws. So, thank you for always bringing this kind of valuable information to your viewers' attention. You are one of this city's real treasures.

TG: Why, thank you, Darwin, that's very kind of you. You know, I have listened to the podcast that you and Walker have recorded, but hearing you speak in person is mind-blowing. That reminds me, all of you watching out there should check out this podcast. It's called *Darwin on Life* and is available wherever you get your podcasts. I have put up a link on the "Community Canvas" webpage to help you find it. So, Darwin, I'm sure it has been quite exciting for Walker to hear what you are thinking, but what has it been like for you to be able to communicate with him and have him understand you?

Darwin: Tina, I have to say, it has taken our relationship to a whole new level. I have always enjoyed Walker's company, but it has been frustrating that our conversations have been so one-sided. Now that he understands what an active life of the mind I have, our interactions are a lot richer. I think I have opened his mind to a whole new way of looking at the world—call it a dog's eye view—and I am sure he agrees that I have really expanded his horizons.

TG: Is that so, Walker? Do you think that talking with Darwin has made you a more interesting person?

WG: Well, I guess you could say that.

TG: Great. So, tell me, how do you propose to build on the research you have done to date? What are your plans for the next few months?

WG: Well, we plan to record a few more—

TG: Sorry, Walker, I was asking Darwin.

WG: Oh, sorry.

TG: Darwin?

Darwin: I'm so glad you asked, Tina. As you can imagine, the kind of research Walker and I are doing can get pretty expensive. So, we are trying to figure out ways to create a sustainable income stream. I'm really hoping our appearance here today will generate more interest in the podcast so that we can attract some major corporate sponsors. In addition to recording more episodes of the podcast, I have a few creative projects in mind that I hope will be successful.

TG: Really? What kinds of creative projects?

Darwin: Well, my neighbors, Rex and Daisy, and I have formed a vocal group, Darwin and the Finches. I am the lead singer, and Rex and Daisy provide backup harmonies. We have an album's worth of pop songs almost ready to release. I am also working on a classical music piece that I hope will get a lot of attention.

TG: That's incredible! So, can Rex and Daisy talk, too?

Darwin: Not to get bogged down in semantics, but all dogs can talk in the sense of communicating through sounds. But to be honest, our attempts to involve other dogs in our experiments have not been entirely successful. So, let's just say that Rex and Daisy's contributions to my musical projects are more in the line of vocalizing than singing, per se.

TG: Fantastic! I can't wait to hear your music.

Darwin: Then there's my memoir. I am taking a few minutes each day to record my thoughts on the day's events. I hope to have enough material for the first volume by the end of the year. If all goes well, I plan to draft a screenplay based on my life story. Can I count on you to take one of the leading roles in the film?

TG: I'd love it! Darwin, would you mind taking a few questions from our audience? I'm sure they all have wondered what their own dogs are thinking, and maybe you can shed some light on that for them.

Darwin: It would be my pleasure.

TG: Terrific! Our first question comes from Terry from Hightown. Go ahead, Terry.

Terry: Thank you, Tina. And good morning, Darwin! You are amazing! My question is this. My dog Bobo is super friendly. But when we go on walks and he sees another dog, he snarls and acts like he wants to attack the other dog. Why does he do this, and how can I get him to stop?

Darwin: Great question, Terry. A dog on a leash behaves very differently from a dog walking freely on its own. That is why I have started a movement called Ditch the Leash to try to liberate my canine friends from this inhumane imposition. I recognize, however, that human society may not be ready yet to cope with total dog freedom.

So, let me tell you what I think is going on. When I see another dog walking with its human companion, I am vigilant to make sure the other dog is not preparing to attack either Walker or me. If I were not on a leash, I could easily approach the other dog until I got within sniffing range. At that point, I could discern whether the other dog was friend or foe and take appropriate action.

If you pull your dog away from the other dog to avoid a conflict, that just reinforces the notion that the other dog is to be feared. Try letting your dog approach the other dog slowly until it gets close enough to pick up its scent. If the other dog reacts calmly, you can introduce them. If not, just go on your way.

Terry: Thanks, Darwin, that sounds like good advice.

TG: Thank you, Terry. Next up is Jerome from Lakeview. Jerome, what is your question?

Jerome: Good morning, Tina. And hello, Darwin. Darwin, how would you say "peanut butter" in dog?

Darwin: Peanut butter.

Jerome: No, I mean in dog language. Oh, wait, I get it. Everything you say gets passed through the app and comes out in English. Sorry, my bad.

Darwin: No problem. But since you mentioned peanut butter, do you have any on you? I love peanut butter. [Audience laughter]

TG: Darwin, you are a riot! OK, we have time for one more question. Meg from Oxbow, what do you want to ask Darwin?

Meg: Thanks, Tina. Darwin, you are absolutely adorable. Do you have a girlfriend?

Darwin: Well, Meg, sorry to be so blunt, but you are not really my type. I prefer someone with a lot more fur. [Audience laughter]

TG: Darwin, you are a hoot! I'm afraid that's all the time we have. I want to thank my guests, Darwin and Wallace—

WG: Walker.

TG: Sorry. Darwin and Walker, for coming on the show. And be sure to check out their podcast, *Darwin on Life*. Goodbye!

Chapter 24

Darwin on Life
Episode 12: Darwin the Philosopher

[Opening theme music]

VO: *Darwin on Life*: Man and dog at the dawn of a new age.

Walker Grant: Hello, and welcome to *Darwin on Life*. I am your host, Walker Grant. I want to extend a special welcome to our new listeners who saw us on the *Coffee and Tina* show. This was the first time either Darwin or I had been on television, and I must say it was an interesting experience. Darwin, what did you think?

Darwin: Most of it was wonderful. Tina was a real sweetheart. She gave me lots of treats and stroked my head just the way I like it.

WG: Yes, you certainly charmed her. She told me afterward that she would like to have us back on the show in a few months to follow up on all the creative projects you mentioned. I think she is seriously hoping to have a major role in the film you talked about. I get the feeling she is eager to break out of this small media market and get more national exposure. But what was it you didn't think was wonderful?

Darwin: As you will recall, when the taping was over, Tina asked us if we could spend a little time chatting with the audience members. Some of them were nice enough, and I had a few interesting discussions about the economy and local politics. But I would estimate that, of the thirty or so people there, about twenty asked me the same question: "Who's a good boy?" I mean, after saying "Me," what more was there to say?

WG: I can understand your frustration. But you were lucky that people wanted to talk to you at all. When I tried to start up a conversation, all people could say was, "What a clever dog you have." No one gave me any credit for coming up with the app that let them hear your thoughts. A few tried to convince me to interview their dogs, but I was able to deflect them. I still have to figure out how things went wrong with Fluffy. She seems to be smart enough, but as you remember, she wasn't very articulate during our interview. In any event, thanks for putting up with all of that so well.

Darwin: No problem. I actually enjoyed all the attention. And the bright lights and cameras didn't bother me as much as I thought they might. I am starting to think I may have a real future in show business.

WG: All right, don't get ahead of yourself. We still have a lot of work to do exploring the outer limits of interspecies communication. Which reminds me, I wanted to get your thoughts on some topics we haven't touched on in previous episodes. There is a fair amount of debate among scientists as to whether animals have true emotions the way humans do. What is your opinion?

Darwin: Well, Walker, as with any scientific inquiry, we first need to agree on definitions. You ask if animals have emotions "the way humans do," which simply begs the question, "What are human emotions?" Are they just recognizable changes in consciousness brought about by external stimuli? If you say, "I'm happy," are you really saying anything more than, "Something just happened that caused my brain to secrete dopamine?"

WG: Say, Darwin, that's a very good point. It sounds like you have studied this issue a lot more than I have. I guess what I was really wondering is whether you are conscious of your own feelings or if your reactions are all merely instinctive.

Darwin: Ah, yes, the old self-awareness question. I'm a little surprised you have to ask. I mean, didn't I tell you how angry I was when you dressed me up like a reindeer on New Year's Eve? And didn't I tell you how happy I am when I visit Penny and Patty's house, where I can play with the other dogs?

WG: Yes, that's true. I think what I am trying to get at is whether you have a personal philosophy that motivates you. For example, have you contemplated your own mortality, and, if so, how does that affect you? Take me. I have worked for years trying to prove that meaningful interspecies communication is possible. Sure, part of my motivation is just to stay employed so that I can provide for myself. And, of course, it has been very gratifying that our experiments have proven the validity of some of my ideas.

But a major reason why I kept at this so long, even in the face of lots of failure and disappointment, was the belief that I could leave a legacy. That something I did would be remembered and appreciated long after I'm gone. I mean, think how some of the geniuses of the past must feel. Think how satisfied Mozart and Beethoven must be knowing that their music is enjoyed by millions, even centuries after their deaths. Imagine how Newton and Einstein and your namesake Darwin feel knowing that their theories still form the basis of their scientific fields. Do dogs aspire to that kind of immortality?

Darwin: Brace yourself, Walker, because I'm afraid I have some bad news for you. Mozart, Beethoven, Newton, Einstein, Darwin, and all the other geniuses don't feel a thing. Do you know why?

WG: Uh, no. Why?

Darwin: Because they're dead. Kaput. Worm food.

WG: Wow! Darwin, I never pegged you for a nihilist. You seem so happy most of the time. Have I misunderstood what is going on with you?

Darwin: Not at all. It is because I don't strive to leave a legacy that I appreciate every moment of life as I live it. Think about it. At best, I have only about fifteen years. What could I possibly achieve in such a short time that would have lasting value? I can't build anything because I don't have opposable thumbs. I can't create a family dynasty for reasons we have discussed before. It's true, now that you have given me the power to communicate with humans, I can at least leave some of my wisdom behind in this podcast. But I am not so vain as to think that what little wisdom I may possess will have any long-term influence.

WG: So, what motivates you to keep going? What impels you to get out of bed every morning?

Darwin: Well, a literal answer to those questions is you. If you didn't wake me up to go on our morning walks, I would happily stay in bed for another few hours of shut-eye. But, seriously, we dogs think of life as a wonderful gift. Every day we get to discover exciting new smells and play with our friends and eat good food. What's not to like?

WG: So, when people say that someone lives a dog's life to mean that he is miserable, they have it all wrong. From what you're saying, a dog's life is pretty sweet.

Darwin: Exactly! You should try it.

WG: It sounds tempting, but how could I? I mean, people have responsibilities.

Darwin: Who says you can't enjoy fulfilling your responsibilities? It all comes down to having the right attitude.

WG: Hmm. You may be on to something. OK, there's one other topic I have been eager to explore. Modern humans tend to find life very stressful and are prone to mental health problems like anxiety and depression. Do dogs have to deal with any of that?

Darwin: Of course. Haven't you seen all the products advertised that claim to treat these conditions in dogs? Pills to relieve separation anxiety and special shirts and dog beds that keep dogs calm during thunderstorms. Anxiety is very common in dogs and is part of what has kept us safe throughout our existence. I know you tease me about my concern with predators, but if dogs didn't have a certain level of anxiety, we wouldn't be so alert to the potential dangers that can befall us.

WG: That makes sense. How about depression? Do dogs ever get the blues?

Darwin: Not really. Sure, we get sad when we lose a family member or close friend. And we can grieve for a long time over such losses. But I think it's fair to say that dogs are more accepting of life's ups and downs. We know instinctively that that's the way life is and that there's nothing we can do about it. So, we go on about our lives looking to get the most enjoyment out of them possible in the short time we have on this earth.

WG: Now I'm starting to think that you are less a nihilist and more an epicurean. Am I right?

Darwin: Frankly, Walker, I think you would be a lot happier if you didn't feel the need to constantly label things. You should, to coin a phrase, "Go with the flow."

WG: Maybe you're right. I guess it's just the scientist in me that wants to categorize everything.

Well, Darwin, we've reached the end of another episode. Thanks again to our listeners, both new and old, for tuning in. See you next time!

Darwin: [Singing]: Eat, drink, and be merry, for tomorrow we may die...

[Outro music; credits]

❦

Chapter 25

March 17, 2024

I can't believe it has been two months since Darwin and I appeared on the *Coffee and Tina* show and even longer since I have had time to write anything in my journal. So much has gone on since then that I'm not sure where to begin.

I suppose the key event that triggered all the activity was the telephone call I received from Pansy Wang. The interview we did on *Coffee and Tina* was noticed by the national network, which showed a short segment of it on its morning program *JBC AM*. Pansy, who identified herself as a talent agent, saw the clip and had a proposal she wished to discuss with me. She said it was somewhat sensitive, so she was reluctant to share any details over the phone. She did say it could prove to be quite lucrative. I was caught completely off guard, so I just took her number and said I would get back to her. She said she understood, but that the proposal had a short shelf life, so I should meet with her as soon as possible.

Diane is the only person I know with any connection to the media sphere, so I called her to get her advice. She told me Pansy Wang was one of the most successful talent agents in the business and that she had a reputation for being both a tough negotiator and a person of unquestioned integrity. So, I called Pansy back, and we agreed to meet in her office in New York a couple of days later. She asked me to bring a printout of the stats from the podcast host site showing how many downloads there had been of each episode of *Darwin on Life*. I asked if I should bring Darwin, and she said that would not be necessary. The whole thing sounded mysterious, but I trusted Diane's recommendation. Besides, I always enjoy visiting New York, and Darwin would have a good time at his sitters' house.

When I arrived at Pansy's building, I took the elevator up to the fortieth floor, where her company was located. I waited in the reception area until Pansy came to escort me to her office. It was a large corner office with an astounding view of downtown Manhattan. The office was sparsely furnished, but several large modern art paintings adorned the walls. Pansy was an attractive, petite woman whom I guessed to be in her late 50s. She asked me to sit at a small table next to one of the windows.

Pansy began by thanking me for coming and asking how Darwin was doing. I assured her he was in good hands and probably having a ball with the other dogs staying with the sitters. She then came straight to the point of our meeting. She had a contact who was on the verge of expanding into the pet food business but had yet to settle on a marketing strategy. The name of the new business would be Howling Beagle. Apparently, the owner of the company had a pet beagle when he was a child and wished to pay tribute to it. They would soon be offering a range of high-end dog food made with fresh meat and vegetables. Customers would order online, and the food would be delivered to their doors in refrigerated vans.

Pansy said she thought she could convince the company to use Darwin as its mascot, but we would have to make a strong case. She asked to see the download stats for *Darwin on Life*. At first, she looked concerned, but when she got to the last page, her eyes lit up.

"Professor Grant," she said, "did you realize that, following Darwin's appearance on *Coffee and Tina*, your downloads went from less than one hundred to over ten thousand? And, that after the clip was shown on *JBC AM*, they jumped to nearly one hundred thousand?"

I said that I had glanced at the numbers but had no idea what they meant. She said they meant that Howling Beagle would be very impressed. Now, she said, the only thing that remained was to do a screen test with Darwin and set up a presentation for her contact at Howling Beagle. She handed me her standard representation contract and recommended that I have an attorney take a look at it. She gave me the names of a few entertainment lawyers who had represented other clients of hers and asked me to get the signed document back to her in the next few days. In the meantime, she would set up a screen test for Darwin.

I got back to my hotel room in a daze but managed to collect myself enough to schedule an appointment with one of the entertainment lawyers. We met the next day, and he agreed to take me on as a client. He told me the contract with Pansy was unexceptional and recommended that I sign it. He also agreed to let me postpone payment of his retainer fee until I had secured the contract with Howling Beagle.

I dropped the signed contract off at Pansy's office and headed back home. Pansy called me the next day to say the screen test was arranged for the following Wednesday. So, a few days later, I was back in New York, this time with Darwin in tow. We stayed in a pet-friendly hotel, which Darwin loved because they handed out lots of treats and he could hang out with some of the other guests' dogs.

We arrived at the studio and met the director, camera crew, and a professional dog trainer who had been hired for the occasion. The director explained how the test would work, and Darwin and I listened attentively. I was afraid Darwin, given his independent streak, might balk at having to take direction from a stranger. But I should have realized that his love of the spotlight and his innate dramatic flair would ensure his cooperation.

The screen test lasted about an hour with Darwin assuming a variety of poses and going through a series of actions: walking toward a food bowl, standing on his hind legs to get a treat, and so on. The crew asked me to set up my laptop so they could record Darwin reciting a few lines of dialogue. The test went smoothly, and the trainer assured me that Darwin was a natural performer who had all the qualities necessary to achieve a successful acting career. Darwin gave the whole crew hugs, which cemented his relationship with them. They said they looked forward to Darwin coming back to film the actual commercials.

A few days later, Pansy called to say she had some good news. The Howling Beagle people had seen the screen test and were thrilled. They wanted Darwin to be their company mascot and to appear in a series of commercials for them. They also agreed to sponsor the *Darwin on Life* podcast. Pansy said she had some other ideas that she wanted to pursue, that she would discuss with me when I came up to sign the contract with Howling Beagle. The company wanted to do a big press event to launch their product line, and they wanted Darwin to take part.

I told her that all sounded wonderful and that I would think it over and get back to her in a few days. The line was silent for a few seconds before Pansy came back on. Her voice took on a steelier tone.

"What is there to think about, Walker? The Howling Beagle people are ready to move. They want to do the press event next week, so they need an answer now."

"But I need to talk to the university," I explained. "I have a seminar that starts next week, and I'm afraid all this publicity business will take a lot of my time. Besides that, I'm worried this will all be a big distraction from my research. I have made so much progress, and I don't want to let that slip away."

"Walker, let me tell you something I have learned over my many years as a talent agent. An opportunity like this comes along at most once in a lifetime. Darwin was a sensation on the *Coffee and Tina* show, but his fifteen minutes of fame will soon come to an end. We need to strike while the iron is hot, or all of this will go up in smoke."

My head was spinning, and I let out a long sigh. I had some real doubts that this was a sensible way to move forward with my scientific work, but I also didn't want to blow what could be my best chance to secure adequate funding. Darwin and I had discussed the advantages of having a corporate sponsor many times, but now that this was a real possibility, I was getting cold feet. Before I could say anything more, Pansy chimed back in.

"I haven't told you yet how much the Howling Beagle people are offering." When she told me, I was flabbergasted. Even the basic contract to advertise on the podcast and for Darwin to do the commercials was more than twice my university salary. Pansy said she negotiated a residuals clause that could keep income coming in for several more months. She also said that her ideas for building on Darwin's celebrity could bring in a lot more revenue.

I felt like a bird in a gilded cage. What Pansy was offering would change my life forever. But was it a change for the better or worse? Whichever decision I made held potential pitfalls. While I was engaged in a furious internal debate, an idea jumped into my mind. I told Pansy I understood the situation and would call her back in fifteen minutes with my decision.

I hooked Darwin up to the computer and relayed the essence of my conversation with Pansy. "Darwin," I told him, "you are the wisest person—well, dog—I know. I really need your advice. Do you think I should sign the contract with Howling Beagle?" Knowing how keen Darwin was to become a celebrity, I assumed he would respond immediately with an enthusiastic "Yes." But he took a few moments to ponder before he answered.

"Walker, I am just a two-year-old dog without a lot of worldly experience. But one thing I have learned is that dreams do not always come true in the way you expect them to. You have spent your whole life trying to communicate with animals. You finally achieved some success, yet no one seems to take your work seriously. With the money you can make from Darwin Enterprises, LLC—I hope you like the name; I've been working on it for some time now—you would be free to devote your attention to your research without having to constantly subjugate yourself to the whims of the university. Sure, this would not be the standard track toward the acceptance you crave, but it would let you pursue your dream without the shackles that have held you back. If you want my opinion, I say, 'Go for it!' As we dogs say, you have to chase squirrels while the sun shines."

I called Pansy back immediately and accepted her proposal. The next day, I met with Dr. Gabor, the chair of the university personnel committee, and told her I would be unable to teach the seminar. I gave her only a cursory description of my planned activities as I feared she would think they were frivolous. Gabor said that finding a replacement to teach the seminar would not be a problem as several graduate teaching assistants were available, any one of whom would be glad to step in. She warned me that she could not guarantee there would be a place for me in the fall if I wished to return, but wished me good luck.

Pansy offered to let Darwin and me stay at her place in Westchester County for several days while we launched our various new ventures. She had a little mother-in-law cottage on the other side of the swimming pool from her elegant mansion. I say "little," but it had more floor space than my townhouse. The entire compound was surrounded by a tall wall, and Pansy said Darwin was free to roam the property at will so long as I picked up his poops and repaired any damage he did to the flower beds. Darwin was thrilled, and he earned his keep by chasing the bunnies that managed to sneak into the yard away from the little greenhouse where Pansy raised vegetables.

The first order of business was to record the commercials for Howling Beagle. The team at the studio was delighted to see Darwin again, and the whole process went without a hitch. They recorded three sixty-second spots, each of which could be cut down to thirty seconds to fit shorter ad buys. All three featured Darwin extolling the virtues of Howling Beagle dog food as he walked through a variety of landscapes and chatted with children. In one sequence, Darwin appeared on a pickleball court and was able to show off his signature serve. Each ad ended with Darwin reciting the slogan, "If your dog could talk, he would ask for Howling Beagle!" followed by a hearty howl.

The product launch was held in a modest-sized auditorium in Manhattan and was attended by reporters and suppliers of the inputs for the Howling Beagle dog food. As the TV ads played on giant screens around the room, wait staff in dog costumes served dog-themed treats to the guests: little hot dogs in tiny buns, mini dog bowls filled with vichyssoise, shortbread in the shape of a dog bone, and other canine-themed delights.

The highlight of the event was a short interview with Darwin. To my surprise, Tina Gray had come up to New York just for this purpose. She really was jumping on the Darwin bandwagon! The Howling Beagle media team had prepared the questions and answers in advance, all of which had Darwin making some kind of humorous commentary—mostly potshots at competing dog food brands. Darwin got the biggest laugh when Tina asked him if he had a girlfriend, and he repeated the line he used on the *Coffee and Tina* show about preferring someone with a lot more fur.

The morning after the launch, Pansy invited me to join her for breakfast in her sunroom. She had several ideas she wanted to run by me that would promote the Darwin brand and bring in additional income. Many of the ideas, she admitted, had come from Darwin himself in the sixth episode of *Darwin on Life*. The first idea was to spruce up the podcast and get it more visibility on the top podcast websites. She said she liked the spontaneity of the originals but thought they could use a little more polish: better sound, new theme music, complete credits at the end, that sort of thing. She also wanted Darwin and me to record a few short promos that could be inserted into other podcasts to try to convince their listeners to check out *Darwin on Life*.

Pansy recommended that we hold off on recording any new *Darwin on Life* episodes until we saw how well the first twelve were received following the brush-up. She said we could re-release one episode a week as we built our new following. That would give us time to decide whether we needed to make any changes to the format. She said several of her other clients had expressed an interest in being guests on our podcast and that this might be a good direction for us to take.

I agreed to hold off on recording any new episodes, partly because I knew Darwin and I would be swamped with all the other activities, but also to give me time to come up with some better ideas. I was afraid that bringing celebrity guests onto the podcast might distract us from its real scientific purpose.

Pansy said the next step would be to build a first-class website where fans could find the podcast as well as lots of pictures of Darwin, a biography, and updates on all of Darwin's activities. The primary purpose of the website, though, would be to sell a wide range of Darwin merchandise. Pansy had to agree with the Howling Beagle people not to sell anything that would compete with their product line, but that still left lots of room for Darwin T-shirts, coffee mugs, picture frames, and dozens of other items all emblazoned with Darwin's likeness and featuring some of his quotes from the podcast.

Pansy's next few ideas struck me as outrageous, but she was so brimming with confidence that I heard her out. She wanted to release an actual Darwin and the Finches album with Darwin's original compositions. She had worked with a producer, Nigel Potter, who had vast experience with unconventional artists. All we had to do was come up with the melodies and lyrics, and he and his team would work out the arrangements. Pansy said this was a fairly low-risk proposal for Nigel's label since most pop songs these days are produced almost entirely on computer. The only people who would have to be paid would be the production team and any additional vocalists. So, Nigel was keen to give it a try. I told Pansy I wasn't sure I could get Rex and Daisy to go along, but she told me not to worry about that. We could pay Mr. and Mrs. Finch a small fee to get them to release any rights they might claim.

Pansy also wanted Darwin to do a series of ASMR videos. I asked her what they were, and she explained that ASMR stood for autonomous sensory meridian response—a tingling sensation around the head that some people get from specific stimuli. ASMR videos are designed to produce that feeling, and there are hundreds of them on social media. They often feature cute animals and people whispering. She thought Darwin, with his soulful brown eyes and deep soothing voice, would be a natural. Pansy would set up a YouTube channel for these videos so they could be monetized.

Finally, Pansy suggested that, once Darwin had a large enough following on social media, he should take advantage of his position to become an influencer. We would keep an eye on the demographics of his fan base and work with companies that wanted to sell products to those consumers. She warned me that this could be risky if a product turned out to be substandard or even dangerous, as this would reflect badly on Darwin. She assured me, however, that she had a lot of experience in this area and would vet the products carefully.

I confessed to Pansy that I was a bit overwhelmed by her presentation, but that it seemed she had thought everything through very carefully, and that I trusted her to look after Darwin's and my interests. I asked her how she got involved in media, and she told me a little of her backstory. She left her native Hong Kong shortly before the transfer of the territory back to China. She studied in England for several years, where she met her husband, an American studying at the London School of Economics. After they married, she moved with him to New York, where they started their first public relations firm together. They split up a few years later, and she got the business as part of the divorce settlement.

I asked what she thought had made her so successful. She admitted she had always been very ambitious and had a calculating streak that she inherited from her mother, who had run a chain of successful restaurants in Hong Kong. She said she had always been a disciple of

Sun Tzu and kept a copy of his book *The Art of War* on her bedside so she could consult it before making any major business moves. One of her favorite quotes of his is "Pretend inferiority and encourage his arrogance." This, she said, had helped her successfully navigate a male-dominated world. It was also why she chose to go by the name Pansy, to lure the people with whom she negotiated into a false sense of security.

I started to tell Pansy some of my own history, but she interrupted me to say that she had to get to her office right away for an important meeting. So, I went back to the cottage to tell Darwin what Pansy and I had discussed. Not surprisingly, he was on board with the whole program and went off to put the finishing touches on the songs for his album.

The ads for Howling Beagle made their first public appearance on the Super Bowl broadcast and were a big hit. I invited Diane and Fluffy to watch the game at our place, and, as usual, I put out some snacks, and Diane brought some very nice wine. When Darwin's ads came on, we all cheered and gave him a big hug. The only sour note was that it was obvious that Darwin's voice had been dubbed. I asked Pansy about this later, and she explained that although Darwin had read his lines very well during the taping, the HB people decided to go with a professional actor. Diane and I agreed that the actor made Darwin sound cartoonish, but Darwin didn't seem fazed.

The day after the Super Bowl, a box arrived from HB with a week's supply of dog food. The accompanying note said that this was a little gift to thank Darwin for his great work, and that we could expect similar packages every week for as long as Darwin's contract remained in effect. I had a good chuckle when I looked at the label of one of the meal packets and discovered that it was described as steak tartare.

Darwin was very pleased, even though I refused to serve him *pommes frites* on the side.

Our new website went up on Super Bowl Sunday to take advantage of the publicity generated by the ads. I listened to the first *Darwin on Life* episode and was impressed by how much more professional it sounded. Over the next several weeks, downloads of the podcast skyrocketed, and we did a very brisk business in Darwin paraphernalia. The T-shirts featuring Darwin mouthing the slogan, "To err is human; to forgive, canine," were the biggest sellers, with the "You can't *lose* with Darwin!" campaign bumper stickers a close second.

The university kindly allowed me to use its first-class recording facilities to make the demo tapes of Darwin's songs. We sent these off to Nigel Potter and waited for him to invite us back to New York to cut the actual album. I was thus dumbfounded to get a call from Pansy a few weeks later, saying that the record was finished and telling us to be in New York the following Monday for the release event. She sent us a link to a pre-release copy of the album with strict instructions not to let anyone else hear it.

Darwin and I sat on the couch and played the album. It opened with a short section of Darwin's choral piece, *A Feather on the Breath of Dog*, which was sung by an *a cappella* children's choir. I thought this was an inspired choice as it built up excitement for what was to follow—a bit reminiscent of the opening of the Rolling Stones song "You Can't Always Get What You Want." The chorale immediately segued into "Scratchin' with My Hind Leg," which Pansy had told us would be the first single released.

The whole recording was very polished, and the arrangements gave the tunes real pizzazz. Once again, however, I was disappointed to hear that Nigel had replaced Darwin's original vocals with those of some professional singers. There were several points where I thought I recognized Darwin's voice in unison with the lead singer and on some of the harmony parts. I thought Darwin would be displeased, but he wagged his tail happily in time with the music.

Pansy apologized later for not giving me a heads-up regarding the substitute vocalists but explained that Nigel had made the decision without consulting her. She told me, however, that she thought he made the right call as the resulting tracks were much more radio-friendly. I said I was afraid we were creating a Milli Vanilli situation that could come back to bite us. Pansy told me not to worry. She said everyone recognizes that, for people to understand him, Darwin's voice must be computer-modified. Using real singers would create a more pleasing sound. She also assured me that the actual singers would be credited and would even appear in the videos for each song. She said I should think of Darwin as the genius behind the project and not focus so much on his vocal performance.

Darwin and I went back to New York and stayed again at Pansy's home. We spent the first day there taping the videos that would be released in conjunction with the songs from the album. Most of the taping, including all the choreographed portions, had already been done, but they still needed several clips of Darwin moving in rhythm to the music and interacting with the singers. Nigel had used three different lead singers, each of whom sang the three or four songs on the album that best suited their style. All three were excited to have the opportunity to get their voices before the listening public, and they all enjoyed frolicking with Darwin.

The record release party was similar to the Howling Beagle product launch, except that all of the attendees were from the music industry and press. Several musicians who had worked with Nigel in the past were there. Since Nigel's specialty was novelty records, I shouldn't have been surprised to see some of the outlandish clothing they wore. In fact, the event seemed more like a costume party than a record release. I noted one guy (or was it a girl) in a gorilla costume, a zombie, a couple disguised as conjoined twins, and a trio dressed up like The Three Stooges. Pansy told me these characters show up at all of Nigel's release parties in hopes of being spotted by someone who will remember their one hit and give them another chance to grab the brass ring.

On our last day in New York, Darwin recorded a couple of the ASMR videos. In the first one, a woman from a pet spa gave Darwin a shampoo, carefully dried him off, then brushed his fur very slowly. She asked Darwin in a gentle whisper how he was enjoying each step of the process, and Darwin responded in a similar soft tone. In the other video, Darwin simply stared into the camera while speaking very slowly and softly about how he spends his day. Candles glowed in the background while vaguely new age music played.

The Darwin and the Finches album, entitled *Scratchin'*, was a modest chart success. The first single, "Scratchin' with My Hind Leg," reached number fifteen on the Billboard Hot 100. The video that accompanied the single, however, became a viral hit on YouTube. The choreographer for the video had the dancers reach behind themselves to grab their uplifted feet and use them to scratch their backs. The move, which became known as "the Scratch," turned out to be very popular at dance clubs, with dancers competing to see how high up they could scratch their backs with their feet. The Scratch also became a popular activity at children's birthday parties, which led to a steady stream of revenue from downloads of the song.

A couple of other songs from the album also charted. The rap "Get Out of My Way (I Ain't No Prey)" got some airtime on hip-hop stations and was later used as the background music for an anti-bullying campaign. The tender love ballad "My Furry Valentine" was especially popular with preteen girls. Darwin fans picked up on the fact that it was dedicated to Fluffy, thanks to the lyrics in the second verse:

You're my furry Valentine, and I'll tell you what,
I get a special frisson when I sniff your butt.

The use of the word "frisson" called to mind bichon frise, Fluffy's breed.

With Darwin's celebrity well established, Pansy launched Instagram and TikTok channels where Darwin could post his influencer videos. Darwin enjoyed modeling the harnesses and collars, but had to be talked into wearing anything resembling a costume. A company that makes dog trailers to attach to bicycles let him keep the model he used for the video. Darwin was thrilled, and we now try to get out for a long bike ride at least once a week. Darwin was even asked to promote a line of pickleball equipment. All the brands Darwin recommenced were tagged in the videos, which created yet another income stream for us.

The next big event on our calendar is a cable TV show called *Root on STEM*. It is hosted by a stand-up comedian named Joshua Root, who studied to be an astrophysicist before turning to comedy. Root invites a mixed group of scientists and showbiz personalities to discuss a variety of STEM-related topics. Much of the discussion revolves around the possible impacts of new scientific findings on daily life as well as their ethical implications. Root chooses his guests carefully to keep the level of discussion remarkably high for a popular television program while still maintaining a light and often very humorous vibe.

The show to which Darwin and I have been invited will focus on artificial intelligence. I am particularly looking forward to meeting one of the guests, Dr. Gordon Highsmith, a leading authority on AI who teaches at Oxford University. I hope to pick his brain on possible fruitful avenues for my future research into interspecies communication.

❧

Chapter 26

October 12, 2024

My therapist suggested I take up my journal again. He says writing about the trauma that led to their depression helps some of his patients with their recovery. I have been putting it off for several weeks, but I realized that we were coming up on the anniversary of my first recorded conversation with Darwin. Today, then, is as good a day as any to give this a try.

I see from my last entry that it was written shortly before the taping of the *Root on STEM* program. The show itself went fine, although I was surprised that, instead of participating in the discussion with the other guests, Darwin and I were asked to come on at the end of the program so that Root could do an interview with Darwin. The topic of the show was artificial intelligence, and even though I was disappointed not to be part of the panel, I enjoyed hearing the discussion among the guests. Dr. Highsmith's descriptions of some of the latest research using AI were especially interesting. My ears pricked up when he mentioned that he would soon be organizing a symposium for AI experts from around the world to discuss their findings.

The guests were amazed, but also somewhat alarmed, by what AI held in store. They made several mildly off-color jokes about the uses they could make of the new technology, but also commented on how they feared that AI would put them out of a job.

When Darwin and I came on, Root asked Darwin several questions we had heard any number of times before: what was it like to be the world's first talking dog, were his dog friends jealous of his fame, and so on. Root asked Darwin if he was afraid that AI might cause him to lose his job. Darwin responded, "Joshua, all this media stuff I do for fun. My job, however, is chasing squirrels, and I don't think AI would be interested in doing that!" This got a big laugh from the panel as well as from the studio audience.

After the show, I buttonholed Dr. Highsmith and asked him if I might be able to participate in the AI symposium he was organizing. He gave a little chuckle and said that the event was a strictly scientific affair, and that there were no plans for any entertainment. He suggested I contact the hotel where the attendees would be staying to see if they had a lounge where Darwin and I could do our act in the evening. He said he thought the participants in the symposium would probably enjoy it.

I was completely confused and assumed that Dr. Highsmith had misunderstood me. So, I told him that I was preparing a paper on my research and that it would be a great opportunity for me to be able to present it at his symposium. Dr. Highsmith looked a little irritated, but before he responded, he paused. He looked me straight in the eyes, and then his gaze softened.

"My goodness," he said, "you honestly believe that your dog can talk, don't you?"

"Of course," I answered, "you just heard him yourself."

"I heard a voice coming from your computer, but I did not hear a talking dog."

I started to get a queasy feeling in my stomach, and I could feel myself starting to sweat. "What do you mean?" I stammered.

"You claim to have invented an app that converts dog sounds to human speech, is that right?"

"Yes," I replied.

"But according to the little bio that you prepared for this show, you do not have a background in computer science. Your degree is in, if I recall correctly, communications studies. How then did you manage to develop a sophisticated AI app without any training in that field?"

"Well, I can do some coding." My sweating was becoming more profuse. "Maybe I shouldn't have used the word 'invented.' I'm not sure what constitutes an invention in the software field. Would 'adapted an app' be more accurate?"

"Perhaps," he replied. "Let me guess. You found an open-source AI app that you downloaded onto your computer, where you gave it access to your database of dog sounds. Am I on the right track?"

"Um, yes," I conceded.

"Do you remember the name of the app you adapted?"

"I'm not sure. I think it started with a C. CESBOT or something like that."

"Might it have been CEPBOT?"

"That sounds right. Why do you ask?"

"Professor Grant, you have been something of a naughty boy. CEP-BOT is available only on the dark internet. Do you know what the CEP in CEPBOT stands for?"

"Uh, no. I never bothered to check."

"It stands for Celebrity Erotic Partner. It is designed to create a character using the voice of a famous person with whom the user can have intimate conversations. That's why it's on the dark internet—so the developers can't be found and sued by the celebrities for appropriation of their voices. I'm told that Beyoncé's voice is the most popular, although apparently Margaret Thatcher's voice is a big hit with the S and M crowd."

By this time, my hands were shaking uncontrollably, and I could barely speak. "But, I never did anything like that with it. I just let it interpret Darwin's words."

"I'm sorry, Professor Grant, but you seem to have a very fuzzy notion as to how AI works. It is true that there are apps that can use AI to translate speech from one language to another, but CEPBOT is not very capable in that area. Even if it were, I strongly doubt it could convert dog sounds into speech. Canine communication is a very different kettle of fish from human language. No, Professor Grant, CEPBOT is simply a chatbot. It created a talking dog for you that responded to your needs. I have to say, having heard the dialogue it produced, CEP-BOT did a remarkably good job."

By now, I was in full panic mode, but I tried to come up with some fact that would cast doubt on Highsmith's assertion. "But if Darwin is just a creation of a chatbot," I sputtered, "how did he know so much about me?"

"Simple. CEPBOT had access not only to the internet but to everything on your computer: your emails, your social media accounts, your writings. That's what makes it so popular. It can create a virtual person who seems like a lifelong friend. I am told that, after the initial fascination with having an electronic sex partner, most users end up talking with it about everyday matters."

I tried to come up with a better counterargument to Highsmith's explanation, but I was completely flummoxed. "I feel like such an idiot," I finally muttered, hanging my head in embarrassment.

"Professor Grant, don't be too hard on yourself. Your basic idea, that animals use language that humans might be able to understand, is not that far-fetched. In fact, there are scientists using AI to try to interpret sperm whale clicks, and their initial research suggests that these whales may use a phonetic language not unlike human speech. Other scientists have trained dogs to understand hundreds of verbal commands. Your only mistake was trying to take a shortcut by using an app you didn't understand that produced results that you misinterpreted. In other words, you were barking up the wrong tree."

I looked up at Highsmith, and his smile as he said this was not condescending but rather the smile of someone sharing a joke. Although I was devastated by what he had just told me, I had the presence of mind to recognize his compassion. He could have dismissed me as a total nincompoop, but instead, he let me down as gently as he could. So, I asked him, please, not to tell anyone that I really believed Darwin could talk. He assured me that he would not, but made me make a promise in return. He asked me not to make some big announcement renouncing my work, but instead to let it fade away naturally. He reminded me that a lot of children were enchanted by Darwin and that telling them that he couldn't talk would be like telling them that Father Christmas wasn't real. He said that most adults recognized that Darwin's talking was some kind of trick, so there was no need to make a public confession.

By the time I got home, my head had cleared a little. I was able to face the reality that, as Highsmith implied, I was the only adult fooled by my own discovery. I didn't have to rush to dismantle the small media empire that had formed around Darwin. I just had to be a lot more thoughtful moving forward.

Still, I held out a small hope that Highsmith was wrong and that the CEPBOT app was more capable than he realized. I listened again to the *Darwin on Life* recordings to see if I could find some evidence that these really were Darwin's musings and not just some digital invention. Highsmith said the app used celebrity voices for its avatars, but I didn't recognize the voice of Darwin as that of any famous person.

As I listened closely, however, I did pick up on something I hadn't noticed before. Darwin's speech sounded a little distorted, like when a TV news program camouflages the voice of someone who doesn't want to be identified. So, I tried raising the pitch of the voice a semitone at a time to see what effect it would have. When I got to three semitones higher, I was shocked by what I heard. It was a voice I recognized all too well—mine! All the time I thought I was talking to Darwin, I was really just talking to myself.

October 21, 2024

I have reread my last journal entry several times now, and I think I am at the point where I can stop berating myself for my stupidity long enough to recap what happened after Dr. Highsmith pulled the scales from my eyes. For a couple of weeks, I was too depressed even to leave the house. Fortunately, Darwin had no media obligations during that period, so I didn't have to make any decisions as to what to do next. Diane called a few times to invite us to play pickleball or come over for a glass of wine, but I put her off, claiming to be suffering too much from seasonal allergies.

Even though I was not engaged with it, the Darwin media juggernaut plowed ahead at full steam. The *Darwin on Life* podcast audience expanded as each episode was re-released on the website, and sales of Darwin-themed merchandise grew proportionally. Howling Beagle dog food proved to be a great success, and the ads ran frequently. The ASMR and influencer videos continued to get large numbers of views, and the Darwin and the Finches album remained popular on music download sites. In short, we were making money hand over fist without having to do a thing.

I thought about the last thing Dr. Highsmith had told me—that most adults recognized that Darwin wasn't really talking—and it slowly dawned on me that although I was clearly not a great scientist, I lucked into being a successful entertainer. I contemplated just carrying on having Darwin do more ads, recording more videos and songs, and making occasional TV appearances. But I soon realized that my heart wouldn't be in it. The only thing that had made this whole media circus worthwhile for me was the belief that I was giving Darwin the chance to express himself.

After a few more weeks of reflection, I still wasn't entirely sure what I wanted to do with the rest of my life, but I knew I didn't want to keep churning out content for the Darwin media machine. As Pansy had told me, Darwin's moment in the spotlight was likely to come to an end soon anyway, so that part of the decision was easy. I also couldn't face the prospect of returning to the university. I had grown weary of teaching, and the administration never really made me feel welcome there. I also knew that if I stayed where I was, I would be constantly reminded of my botched effort to achieve communication with Darwin.

I called Diane and asked her if she could come over for lunch. As we nibbled on salad niçoise and sipped a crisp pinot grigio, I told her about my conversation with Dr. Highsmith and how mortified I was that my excitement over communicating with Darwin had blinded me to what was really going on. I asked her if she knew all along that Darwin wasn't really speaking.

Diane put down her fork, took a sip of wine, and told me, "Walker, I am no expert on computers or AI or even dogs. It did seem a little odd to me, though, that a dog would use such sophisticated language. But you seemed so sincere that I didn't give too much thought to the matter. When I got to see Darwin speaking on the *Coffee and Tina* show, though, I thought I noticed that words were coming out of the computer even at times when it wasn't clear that Darwin was making any sound. I probably should have asked you about it at the time, but we hadn't been friends for very long at that point, and I didn't want to say anything that might upset you."

I tried to think of a response, but all I could focus on was the fact that Diane had called me her friend. I finally just thanked her for her sensitivity and asked her if it would be all right if I consulted with her over the next few weeks as I tried to figure out what to do next.

She said, "Of course," and we finished our lunch talking about nothing more momentous than what mischief Fluffy and Darwin had gotten into lately.

A few days after my lunch with Diane, and after a few phone calls with her to get her opinion, I decided to make a radical change that would give me time to think through what was truly important to me in life. With some of the profits from Darwin Enterprises, I bought a small farm about a two-hour drive away. I spent a little more money to outfit the old farmhouse with modern plumbing and electricity, and installed a satellite dish so we could get internet and TV. Most importantly, I fenced in the acre of land right behind the house to give Darwin a lot of space to roam around in. We have been here a couple of months now, and I think we are going to like it.

July 4, 2025

Happy Independence Day! I no longer feel the need to keep up this journal, but I thought I would make one last entry to bring the saga of Darwin the talking dog to a close. It obviously won't be of any use to scientists, but maybe it can serve as a cautionary tale to my nieces and nephews. I will print out a few copies and, if they ever ask me about my glory days as a media personality, I will hand it to them with instructions to read it carefully.

My new life is not the result of me forming and implementing a specific plan but rather of letting life happen and grabbing at the best of it as it floats by. I have gotten to know the people in the small town about a mile from our house, and they seem to have accepted me as a friendly, if rather eccentric, presence. Having Darwin with me is a big help in breaking the ice, as no one can resist his charms.

I discovered that one of my new neighbors has a small factory where he produces goat cheese that he sells to restaurants in the city. He wanted to expand his business and suggested that, since I had a barn and plenty of pasture, I raise some goats for their milk. I did a little research and concluded that goat farming would not be insuperably difficult. I went to a local farm that had some goats for sale to see what I would be getting myself into. Seeing the goats' sweet faces and watching the kids frolic around their pen won me over. So, I gave it a go. We currently have eight goats and will probably add a few more as we get more experience.

I realize I am saying "we," as I still think of Darwin as my partner. He can't really herd the goats, but he does like chasing them around the field, which gives them some exercise. I should mention that we picked up another dog at the local shelter. He is a mixed breed, about the same age as Darwin, and I'm happy to say the two get along like gangbusters. I named him Newton to keep up the science theme. Having a playmate for Darwin works well for me when I need to spend a little quiet time alone. I can just kick those two out to the backyard while I read a book, listen to some music, or take a nap, and they keep themselves amused for long stretches at a time.

The best part about having a country place, though, is that people like to come and visit, and I have plenty of room to accommodate them. My sister Gina has been here several times, and we have a lot of fun reminiscing about our childhood. She brings food items from the city that are hard to find here and always cooks up a grand feast. Her husband, Mel, is happy to show off his carpentry skills and has helped me make several improvements to the farmhouse and barn. Gina's children adore Darwin and Newton and spend hours scampering with them in the field behind the house.

Even my brother Kyle and his family stopped by on their way to check out some wineries in the neighboring valley. They were surprisingly complimentary about the farm and said they would talk up the goat cheese when they got back home. Kyle is considerably less condescending toward me now that I have had my own brush with fame and fortune.

Best of all, Diane and Fluffy visit almost every weekend. Diane loves the peace and quiet, and Fluffy enjoys having two beaux that she can play off each other. I am thinking of building a pickleball court behind the barn to give us something else to do. But the time seems to fly by when Diane is here, so there's no rush. There's no rush with our relationship either—we just enjoy the time we spend together without having to think too hard about what might come next.

Darwin still likes to sit next to me on the sofa while we watch *Jeopardy!* after supper. He rubs his head against my chest and looks up at me with his warm, brown eyes. It's his way of telling me...well, I guess I'll never know.

Acknowledgments

I wish to thank my extraordinarily talented editor, Annie Jo Smith, for turning this mangy mutt of a novel into a well-groomed show dog. Thanks also to my dear friend, Anna Flaaten, for introducing me to Annie Jo and for encouraging me in my writing journey.

About the Author

Gary Clements is a retired lawyer and diplomat who lives in Chapel Hill, North Carolina, with his pet beagle Darwin. *Darwin Speaks!* is his first novel. He is currently working on a children's book that also features Darwin, and a musical inspired by his Foreign Service career.